# OLD HICKORY'S PRISONER

THE TRACKS IN THE EARTH AND LEAVES LED DOWN THE GLEN.

# OLD HICKORY'S PRISONER

## A TALE OF THE SECOND
## WAR FOR INDEPENDENCE

BY

### BERNARD MARSHALL

AUTHOR OF "THE TORCH BEARERS,"
"REDCOAT AND MINUTE MAN," ETC.

## D. APPLETON AND COMPANY
### NEW YORK :: LONDON :: MCMXXV

# CONTENTS

# ILLUSTRATIONS

# OLD HICKORY'S PRISONER

## CHAPTER I

### SWINGING LANTERNS

A BITING, northeast wind surged and howled through the streets and along the docks of the little New England town, and a gray and cloud-filled sky frowned down upon it with only a few flickering stars dimly visible in the yellowish haze to the west. The feeble flames of the lanterns on the sides of the main thoroughfare and in front of the old Court House at its head leaped and shimmered in the gale, threatening every moment to expire and leave the cobble-paved ways in utter darkness. The ground was bare of snow, but thick films of ice already covered the puddles in the gutters and alley ways. Save for a few slowly moving specks of light, the waters of the river and of the harbor below were black as ink.

Altogether, the evening of the twelfth of December in the year 1813 was hardly one to invite the sober inhabitants of New London to leave their snug firesides and walk abroad, to say nothing of assembling on the gusty street corners and upon the blackened and half

I

ruined docks, in wait for a spectacle. Yet that was their employment, almost to the last man, woman and child. Granny Beecher of the State Street Toy Shop was kept at home by her rheumatism, and old Foxon, the revolutionary veteran with the wooden leg, who was sexton at the First Orthodox Church, had not yet appeared on the street; but Will Brewster, the minister's son, had twice declared to his cousin, Hubert Delaroche, that every other person in town was abroad and among the sightseers. Many of them shivered and stamped their feet or threshed their arms about while they waited; and Billy Jamaica, Cap'n Doble's negro lad, danced a jig on the paving stones, to the scandal of many; but none spoke of going homeward or offered to leave any points of vantage they had gained.

It was only at early candle light that word had gone about that Commodore Decatur with his squadron, the United States, the captured Macedonian and the Hornet, would leave the harbor that night in the effort to run the gauntlet of British cruisers that awaited him in the sound below. Some unusual activity had been observed on the American ships in the late afternoon, as they lay in the stream off the Market Wharf; and just at dusk a jack-tar had come ashore to say good-by to his sweetheart. She must have been active in telling what she had learned, for now the whole town was agog with the news. Within three hours Decatur, with his brave little fleet, would be safely out on the broad Atlantic, beginning another glorious cruise that would surely end in victory and the capture of more enemy ships, or, if aught went amiss with his plans, he would be fighting in the waters just beyond the harbor entrance a deathly battle with a force three times as strong as his own. Little wonder that no one in New London had any thoughts of bed or fireside!

Hubert and Will had been racing about from one to another of the groups of watchers for half an hour or more. Twice over they had been convinced that the dim lights out on the black expanse before them were moving toward the sea; and on both occasions Will had shrilly announced to the bystanders that the cruise was begun, only to be compelled to acknowledge a few minutes later that the position of the ships' lanterns still bore the same relation as before to the lines of the dock on which they stood. But now Hubert Delaroche suddenly announced:

"There they go! I see them move for certain."

"You're right," said an old boatman, "they've swung past the line of the smack there. They're off at last."

"We can see nothing of the ships themselves from here," said Hubert to his companion. "Let's go down to Hurley's wharf. 'Twill be lighter there."

At once Will jumped down from the cask on which he had been standing and started on a run for this new location with Hubert close behind. In front of Hurley's the harbor was wider, and now, more light coming from the clouded sky, they were able to make out the masts and sails of the two frigates and the sloop of

3

war that were moving unmistakably toward the open sound.

Hubert was a broad-chested, sturdy-legged lad of sixteen who had come to New London but three months before from his birthplace at Cedricswold in the Connecticut Valley to carry on his studies of Latin and mathematics in preparation for entering Harvard College the following year. He had not clearly understood why the schools at Carrington Village near his home were not ample for this purpose, but being fond of the sea and all that pertained to it, and never having had his fill of boats and sails and oars, he had welcomed this opportunity for a stay at a place where they were every day to be had and used. Under the tutelage of the Reverend William Brewster, his father's cousin, he had made good progress at the books also, so that his parents, who had visited at the Brewsters' but the week before, were well satisfied as to the wisdom of the arrangement for Hubert's schooling.

The truth was that a group of fiery young patriots at Carrington, including a number of Hubert's schoolmates a few years older than himself, were organizing an infantry company to join the army on the Canadian border; and Richard Delaroche and his wife had no desire to see Hubert drawn into the enterprise. The elder Delaroche had fought all through the Revolutionary War and been twice severely wounded. His eldest son, Richard, was already a lieutenant, serving under General Harrison, and the second boy, Myles, a midshipman in Perry's fleet on Lake Erie. Dorothy, the daughter of the house, had postponed her marriage and was helping to nurse the wounded in a hospital at Boston. Under these circumstances the veteran felt that he could scarcely be blamed for wishing to have the youngest of his children go on with his studies at school and college rather than join the colors for what seemed likely to be a long and bitter war. Accordingly he had done his best to banish war talk from the table and fireside at Cedricswold, and, with the eager connivance of the lad's mother, had seized the first opportunity to place Hubert in a household where all the personal influence would be exerted in the opposite direction.

The excellent Mr. Brewster was a Peace Party man. For years he had preached at and argued with his parishioners on the blind obstinacy of President Jefferson and his fellow Democrats in avoiding an alliance with England, the mother country, against the menacing power of France. And even now, in the midst of war with England, he did not fail to offer up prayers night and morning that the eyes of those in authority in the nation's affairs might be opened to the folly and sin of their course. This factious quarrel between the English-speaking nations, he stoutly maintained, was one in which success for America could only mean the triumph of Bonaparte and the downfall of law and righteousness.

Will Brewster was two years younger than his

cousin, and much more slightly built. His voice was still a boyish treble, while Hubert's had settled to a resonant bass that well matched his broad shoulders and manly bearing. Now the younger boy's face looked pinched and pale in the starlight, and he trembled with cold in spite of all their running about which should have amply warmed his blood. His large, dark eyes shone brightly with excitement, and he was far too uneasy to remain in one spot, whatever its advantages as a lookout post, for more than a minute or two at a time. Young Delaroche was no less acted upon by his anticipation of what the next few hours would bring to pass; but the evidences of his state of mind were of a far different sort.

"Come on!" he shouted hoarsely, springing up from his seat on a coil of rope. "I know what we'll do. We'll go out to the headlands and see if they get by the Britishers."

But at this reckless proposal Will's teeth fairly chattered. "I was afraid you'd want to do somethin' like that," he faltered. "Don't let's go out there. It's too cold."

"Too cold!" snorted Hubert. "What's that got to do with it? If there's going to be a battle, don't you want to see it?"

"Ye-es, but I tell *you*, Hubert Delaroche, if there is a battle with all those ships, there'll be a whole lot of cannon balls and grape shot flying 'round. And just

6

as likely as not some of it will come up on the headland."

"Nonsense! There's not one chance in a thousand. And I believe Commodore Decatur is going to do to those Britishers just what Perry did to 'em on Lake Erie. And you can believe I'm going to see it. Now come along if you want to, or go home and go to bed."

Forthwith he started away at a rapid pace; and after half a minute of hesitation the other ran after and caught up with him. They exchanged no more words, and, indeed, Hubert set so fast a pace that Will found need for all his breath in keeping up with him and could spare none for further remonstrances. Three or four other young men and boys joined them on the outskirts of the town; and as they emerged upon the higher open ground they perceived several other groups, coming from different directions and evidently bound on the same errand.

They had traversed perhaps a mile of rough and stony ground, and by alternate walking and running were fairly keeping pace with the squadron, when Will, who had fallen a little way behind, called out excitedly to Hubert to wait for him.

"Oh, what's the trouble?" answered the elder impatiently. "This is no time for waiting. Don't you see they'll be in the Sound in twenty minutes?"

"Look! Look there!" gasped Will, as he overtook his companion. "See that, over on the other side."

Hubert stopped and looked where the boy was point-

7.

ing. A bright, blue light was burning on the opposite headland. The flame seemed to be but a low one, but very bright and steady. Hubert could not remember ever having seen the like.

Then something caused him to turn and look again toward the headland they had been approaching. There was another light, the counterpart of the first. Both of them had been so placed as to be hidden by intervening rocks from any observers in the town or the harbor, but they would be visible for many miles out at sea.

The boys were stumbling forward again, when, mounting a little rise, they saw before them that which made them halt in their tracks. Out in the sound, scarcely a half mile from the harbor entrance, was a broken row of lights that stretched across from side to side and dipped and swung with the motion of the sea. Dimly to be seen around them, after the first few seconds of gazing, were the ghostly forms of ships of war.

"Four! five! six! seven!" counted Will. "Oh, say!" he went on tremulously, "those must be the British fleet. They've come way in—closer than ever. Now I don't care what you say, I'm going home."

"Go on then," answered Hubert, savagely, "I've not come this far to see a battle and then to run home before a shot's fired. But hold now! Our ships are not coming on."

It was true. The lights on the American squadron

had all been extinguished, but the masts and sails were still visible, and these described uncertain motions as the courses of the vessels were rapidly altered. The sounds of shouted commands reached the shore, though not with sufficient clearness to enable the watchers to catch the words. Chains rattled, yards were hauled, and slackened sails flapped in the wind. Soon it was clear that the vessels were putting about and returning toward the anchorages they had left scarcely an hour before.

Commodore Decatur, it seemed, had been foiled in his attempt to slip past the blockading fleet; and neither battle nor escape would be seen that night. Puzzled and disappointed, and stumbling sorely over the pasture rocks and brambles, the two youths made their way back to the town.

## CHAPTER II

## HEADLONG HUGH

THE next afternoon Hubert and his cousin were again on the streets. The Reverend Mr. Brewster had departed three or four days before for a week's stay at New Haven; and the boys were having a holiday from their lessons. Hubert had spent the morning on the harbor, in a sailboat with some older lads; but no plan of equal interest seemed to present itself for the remainder of the day.

"I tell you," he said, as they strolled aimlessly toward the western outskirts of the town, "let's go up to the Windoms'. I'd like to have another game of chess."

But Will halted suddenly, his face registering acute alarm. "Oh, no!" he said quickly. "We don't want to go *there*—not to-day."

"Well, what are you 'fraid of *now?* There won't be any battle out at Mr. Windom's, I hope."

"Won't there?" shrilled Will. "I'm not so sure there won't be. You just wait till you hear what I heard this morning."

"Well, what *did* you hear?"

"Come over here in this shed, and I'll tell you," said Will in a half whisper. "I been meaning to tell you just as soon's we got where no one could hear us."

Hubert led the way to an old lumber shed in the rear of an open lot next the wagon maker's. As soon as they were safely out of sight and hearing Will began:

"I went up towards Windom's this morning. I *didn't go* there exactly; but John MacBean—you know the fellow they call 'Rowdy'?"

"Yes, I've seen him."

"Well, Rowdy MacBean, he stopped me in the road there, and asked me if I'd been to Windom's. I said 'no' I hadn't, and I hadn't either. I'd just been going past there, kind of—"

"I know—looking to see if you could see Margaret at a window."

"I hadn't neither. *I* don't care anything about Margaret. She's too smart and uppity for me. But, any way, I said I hadn't been there; and Rowdy MacBean he said it was lucky for me if I hadn't because if he thought I had he'd break every bone in my body."

"He would, would he?" exclaimed Hubert. "Maybe if I happened to be along, he'd have some one else's bones to break first that wouldn't be so easy."

"Sh-h-h-h! I say, Hubert, *don't* make so much noise. Somebody'll hear you."

"Oh, bother the noise! What's the matter with Rowdy? Why should he pitch on you for going to the Windoms'?"

"Just wait till you hear the reason," whispered Will. "There's more in it than Rowdy MacBean. There's

Bill Sampson and Shorty Molloy and a lot of others. And I tell you I'm scared of 'em. They say that Mr. Lucas Windom is a British spy."

"A British spy? Whoever heard of such a thing?"

"Yes, sir, that's what they say. He's always been a Peace Party man, and so's my father. That's why they pitch on me so quick—and you too. They said if they saw either one of us going near Windom's, they'd break our bones."

"Well, maybe some one else will do some bone breaking if it comes to that. But what's set them to thinking Mr. Windom's a spy? I know he talks against the war hard enough—and no wonder. He was a rich man in Boston before the war shut up his ships in the harbor. But has anybody seen or heard anything that makes him seem a spy?"

"Listen. You know last night we saw those blue lights."

"Yes."

"And the Britishers came way up, almost into the harbor, and stopped our ships from getting out."

"Yes, so it seemed."

"Well, they're saying now that those blue lights were *signals*—that some one on shore who'd learned the commodore was going to sail went and burned those lights to tell the Britishers."

"Well," said Hubert, slowly, "that might *be*. Thinking of it now, it seems mighty likely. But what has all this to do with Mr. Windom?"

"Last night, after we turned 'round and came home, there was one crowd that went clear on down to the point. Rowdy MacBean was with 'em. The blue lights were all out by that time, but they wanted to find out just where they'd been burning. And they met Mr. Windom coming back from there."

"Oh pshaw! What if they did? Mr. Windom probably went down there to see what he could see, just the same as we did."

"Maybe so. But they don't look at it that way. Rowdy says 't the crowd didn't make out just what he'd been up to till this morning. They didn't think quick enough. If they had, they'd have *hung* him right then and there."

"Oh, nonsense! I guess they *would*. Young fellows like that!"

"Well, Rowdy's nineteen, and he's as big as most any man. So's Bill Sampson. And Mr. Jonas White, the blacksmith, was with 'em, too. He's the one that said that about hanging Mr. Windom."

"Oh, they're just talking big to hear themselves talk. They wouldn't do anything of the kind. And I don't believe Mr. Windom's done anything wrong either. He's too much of a gentleman."

"Maybe he hasn't; but he certainly does want this war to stop. *I* know that."

"So do I know it. But that's a very different thing from trying to get our ships destroyed or captured. I don't believe he'd think of such a thing."

"Well, anyway," went on Will with a sigh, "we'd better keep away from there until folks have forgotten about this. We can't fight that whole crowd."

"Keep away?" echoed Hubert. "Do you know what I'm going to do? I'm going out to Windom's right now."

"You are?" questioned the younger lad with wide-open, fearstruck eyes. "Why! you'll just get your head broken; that's what you'll get."

"I'm going up to the Windoms' right now," declared Hubert. "Mr. Windom's the best chess player I ever played with. He's the only one I ever saw who could beat my father. I want to play with him every time I can. Then maybe when I go back home I can beat father myself."

"Oh, yes, you *do* want to play chess," jeered Will. "I think there's somebody else lives in that house besides Mr. Windom."

"If you mean Margaret," answered Hubert, gravely, although with reddening cheeks and ears, "I think nothing of her, for though she's a bright girl, no doubt, and may turn out well enough when she's grown, she's scarcely more than a child now. Fifteen years old or thereabouts. She's more nearly a playfellow for you."

"She thinks nothing at all of me any more since you've come about," blurted Will. " 'Tis much as ever she hears anything I'm saying when you're in the room. You've fairly bewitched her."

14

"Nonsense!" returned Hubert, loftily. "I've done nothing of the sort. I've scarcely looked at her."

"Well, whatever 'tis you go for, you're no better than a fool to go to the Windoms' now. I guess your father was right when he told us the nickname they had for you at Cedricswold."

"What was that?"

"Headlong Hugh."

Hubert threw back his head and laughed. " 'Tis true," he answered finally. "My father so named me after I'd nearly got myself smothered in a quagmire and then had broken an arm in breaking my colt, Mad Anthony, to saddle, all in the same summer. He says I always leap before I look."

"Yes, I believe it. That's what you're doing now."

"No, it isn't. I've looked enough. I know Rowdy and all his crew for big talkers and little doers. 'Tis a month now that they've been talking of beating old Constable Madden for taking up one of their crew and lodging him for a night in the jail; but I don't hear anything of their doing it. 'Twill be the same in this matter of Windom—much talk and little else."

Then, with squared shoulders and head held high as though on parade, Hubert marched out of the shed and turned up the road toward the Windom place. As he went he whistled a gay marching tune and never deigned a glance to left or right to learn whether any one were observing him.

# CHAPTER III

## ROWDY MacBEAN

THE door of the Windom house was opened by the master himself. Though the old, white-painted mansion was large and surrounded by extensive gardens, Mr. Windom kept no servants—he and his daughter making up the entire household. The grounds were much neglected and the green blinds tightly drawn over most of the windows; but in the library—to which apartment Hubert was ushered with some ceremony—a cheerful fire of logs was burning in the grate, the books and furniture were tastefully arranged and the thick maroon carpet and hangings were wholly free from dust or stain.

Lucas Windom was a tall and somewhat corpulent man of forty-five or more, with the dignified and impressive manner of one long accustomed to direct the activities of others. His voice was low but clear and his pronunciation avoided without effort the Yankeeisms that disfigured the speech of most of his neighbors. He never spoke of the *taown* or the *caows*, of *sody* or *neuralgy*, or of *runnin'* or *goin'*; and Hubert, who was accustomed to good English speech at Cedricswold and at the Brewster home, had early noted this

16

distinction on the part of the merchant and that his daughter Margaret shared it.

Mr. Windom's eyes were gray, and, by habit, rather cold and stern, though capable of lighting up surprisingly at any witty thrust in conversation, whether his own or another's, or when they rested in approval on his daughter's face. Iron-gray hair hung in graceful curls over his neckcloth, and, in defiance of the custom, a heavy beard and mustaches covered his mouth and chin. His coat and pantaloons were of dark blue broadcloth and well tailored, though showing now some degree of wear at the seams; his waistcoat was spotless and his boots well polished. Altogether, Mr. Windom was in appearance a gentleman and man of affairs—a personage to command respect in almost any gathering.

The chessboard was produced at once, and soon a game was in progress. The merchant's manner was as gravely deliberate as usual, and he opened the play with his well-known confidence and skill. But after the first ten or twelve moves Hubert, much to his own surprise, managed to increase the initial handicap of a knight that had been granted him by capturing one of his opponent's castles with the sacrifice of nothing more valuable than a pawn. With his hopes greatly roused by this success, he carried the game boldly into the other's king row, seized every opportunity the game afforded for even exchanges, and finally ended with a triumphant checkmate when only six pieces were left on the board.

Hubert was mightily elated with this, his first, victory, but Mr. Windom seemed scarcely to notice it, and, indeed, to be far away in thought as he slowly replaced his pieces on the board. Margaret had entered with some cakes and cider for the players' refreshment, and, after greeting Hubert cordially, had seated herself in a great armchair nearby with her fancy work.

She was a sturdy, well-grown lass with large black eyes, broad, full-lipped mouth and handsome, pointed chin. Her movements were quick and decided, with more than a hint of boyishness, which quality was accented by a most quaint and unusual method of wearing her dark, curly hair. This was cut squarely at the back of her neck, after a fashion prevalent enough in the Low Countries, where she had spent two years at school, but practically unknown in New England. The sampler on which she was engaged represented a row of low-eaved houses, and a windmill, overhanging a canal.

Mr. Windom paused before all his pieces were reset, and, drumming absently on the board with a pawn, sat gazing out of the window.

"I see that Commodore Decatur did not sail out of the harbor last night as he proposed," he said, slowly.

"No, sir," answered Hubert, the game in a moment forgotten, "the British ships came in almost to the harbor mouth, and so blockaded him."

"I wonder he did not sail out and knock them to

18

pieces," went on the merchant, "as we have heard he was likely to do."

"Their fleet was more than twice as strong as ours," answered Hubert, his spirit rising a little at what seemed a covert sneer. "If he had sailed out, 'twould only have been to be defeated."

"In that he doubtless showed good judgment," answered the elder, slowly, "far better than President Madison has shown."

"How so?" demanded Hubert.

"Oh, father!" put in Margaret, "let's not talk of war and politics to-day. Mr. Delaroche sees these things so differently from us that we'll be sure to quarrel."

"Master Delaroche," answered her father firmly, "is a young man of intelligence and some reading—far different from most of these villagers; and he is quite capable of seeing these questions more broadly than they do."

"President Madison, young sir," he went on, "has been guilty of an even greater folly than that of which Commodore Decatur would have been guilty had he sailed out into the Sound last night. He has challenged a power that has a thousand ships of war against our beggarly dozen or so, and that has great armies, well drilled and equipped—veterans of half a hundred European battlefields—to oppose to our scattered regiments of raw and half-armed militiamen. That power even now controls Canada, the Mississippi Valley, the

Gulf of Mexico and the ocean itself—hemming us in on all sides; and it will be able at last to dictate peace to us on its own terms. That's what President Madison and his foolish Democratic advisers have done for us. And if you would make sure what the outcome will be, look at our merchant ships, rotting at the wharves, our handful of warships cooped up in the harbors, behind the forts, like Decatur's here, and our armies defeated in every campaign."

"Even so," replied Hubert, stubbornly, "it hasn't been all one-sided. We've whipped them half a dozen times on the sea in fights between single pairs of ships; and Commodore Perry sunk or captured a whole squadron on Lake Erie."

"Bah! What do those little victories amount to in the general fortunes of war? As any one can see, the British navy rules the seas, and that in the end will decide the issue. And I tell you, Master Delaroche, that we have reason to regret not only the defeats we have suffered but even the victories we have gained. All that they accomplish is to hamper and delay England and her allies in crushing the power of Bonaparte. Had we done our part, that might have been accomplished long before this; and if they make another compromise at Paris and leave that self-serving tyrant on the throne, the blame for it will be ours. If President Madison were well advised, he would seize the first opportunity for negotiating peace with England on the best terms he could get."

"The British kept stopping our ships on the high seas and taking off our seamen."

"Nonsense! Don't believe all the rant the newspapers print about that. That is merely a flimsy excuse, trumped up by the Democrats, for bolstering their policy of war and conquest in the West. The truth is that those fellows who were taken from our ships were nothing more nor less than deserters from the British navy. I am a shipowner, or I *was* before the embargo and this senseless war ruined me, and I know whereof I speak."

To this declaration Hubert could make no adequate reply, for he had never supposed that any legal excuse could be made for the impressment of seamen or for the other indignities the American flag had suffered on the seas. It was evident that Mr. Windom knew far more of the matter than he did, and would certainly best him in an argument. So he turned to the rearrangement of the chessboard, and was glad when Margaret gave the conversation another turn. An hour passed during which, despite his best efforts, he suffered three successive defeats. Then, it being already twilight, he rose and took his leave.

Hubert had walked but little more than a square from the Windom house when John MacBean appeared from behind a hedge at an alleyway and roughly hailed him:

"Hey there, you white-livered Tory! I've got somethin' to say to you."

Hubert wheeled about and faced him.

"You be'n down to the Windom place, hain't you?" demanded MacBean, as he planted himself squarely in the path, with his little, pig-like eyes glaring, his fists doubled and his jaw thrust menacingly forward.

"Well, if I have, what about it?"

"This," snarled MacBean. "I'm goin' to break your pretty nose and wipe up the road with *you*. You had fair warnin', and now I'll show you what happens to Tories and them that stand up for them."

Rushing in like a bull, he aimed a blow at the face of the younger lad that might have been serious had it landed; but Hubert ducked just in time and drove his fist squarely against MacBean's freckled nose. With a furious yell, the other struck out right and left, and the battle was on.

MacBean had the advantage in weight and in length of arm, and might have won fairly if he had kept his head, for he landed twice as many blows as his opponent, and one of these nearly knocked the younger lad off his feet. But one more lucky thrust of Hubert's caught his antagonist full in the face, and in the pain and rage that followed Rowdy completely lost control of himself. Rushing in, and cursing like a pirate, he threw his arms about Hubert's waist and endeavored to throw him to the ground.

He could not have made a worse mistake, for Hubert, who knew but little of boxing and nothing at all of fist fighting save for two or three boyish combats

22

in the schoolyard at Carrington, which had been promptly broken up by the master, was a wrestler whom no youth in the village within thirty pounds of his weight had ever thrown. Now the seemingly ill-matched pair swayed to and fro and whirled about each other for half a minute while Hubert was gaining his favorite hold. Then suddenly MacBean found himself lifted from the ground, whirled sidewise and landed with a crash full on his back in the street, with his antagonist over him, pinning his shoulders to the ground.

There followed desperate efforts on the part of the fallen one to twist himself out of Hubert's grip and to shield his face from blows. But no blows were aimed at him. Instead, young Delaroche was kneeling on his chest, holding him firmly despite all his struggles, and shouting:

"Now *give in*. Give in for beaten, and 'tis over."

Just then the victor heard the sound of running feet and received a tremendous blow on the side of the head that knocked him sprawling on the ground. Mac-Bean scrambled to his feet, and the next instant Hubert was fiercely assailed by two young ruffians at once, and within half a minute was beaten and kicked almost into insensibility. Bill Sampson had glimpsed the combat from a distance, and had run to the rescue of his friend.

Next came the sound of more heavy footsteps and of shouted threats and warnings. For a time Hubert lost all knowledge of his surroundings. When he opened his eyes again, a stout, roughly dressed man was bending over him. In one hand the stranger clutched a heavy, four-foot stick and in the other a tin dipper from which he was pouring cold water. Hubert's face and neck were thoroughly drenched.

"There! Comin' to, be ye?" said the good Samaritan. "Gorry! I'm glad. Thought them young rowdies had killed ye."

Hubert blinked uncertainly for a moment, coughed and choked, then got on hands and knees and slowly rose to his feet. At the side of the road, near the town pump, stood a two-horse wagon with a load of cordwood. His rescuer was evidently the owner.

"Think ye can stand all right?" inquired the farmer.

"Yes," answered Hubert, thickly. "Many thanks to you."

"Wal, I guess they might have finished ye if I hadn't come up when I did. Had to lay on good and hard with this oak stick, too, before they finally cut and run."

"Well, I thank you with all my heart," said Hubert. "And now I'll see if I can wash off some of this blood and dirt."

Unsteadily crossing the street to the pump, he began bathing his face and head with the water in the tub.

The farmer had followed him solicitously. "Hadn't I better take ye home on the wagon?" he said. "How'd you come to git into this fracas?"

24

"Oh, they'd issued orders that I was not to do certain things. And I didn't choose to obey them."

"Wal," said the farmer slowly, "course you don't have to tell me about it if you don't want to. Think you can git home all right?"

"Yes, thank you," replied Hubert, and, having finished bathing his cuts and bruises he dried his face as well as he could with his kerchief, then shook hands with his rescuer and walked away. Following side streets and lanes where he would not be likely to be observed in the growing darkness, he soon made his way back to the Brewster home.

It so happened that neither of his eyes had been blackened in the encounter, and since the worst of the bruises he had suffered were on his legs and body rather than on his face, he did not present too striking a spectacle when he appeared at the supper table. Mrs. Brewster, who was a somewhat absent-minded person at best, had just been elected president of a local society for carrying enlightenment to the Indians, and, full of her new responsibilities, failed to notice anything unusual in the appearance of her husband's pupil. Will's observation, however, was much keener. When the meal was over he followed Hubert to his room and eagerly questioned him on the afternoon's adventure.

Hubert replied with a brief account of what had occurred; and Will listened, wide-eyed and trembling.

"Oh!" he exclaimed at last. "It's lucky they didn't

kill you. And that's what they would have done if that farmer hadn't come along."

"No, I don't believe that," answered Hubert, slowly. "They just wouldn't *dare* to when they couldn't prove anything against me."

"Well, they couldn't prove anything against Mr. Windom, either."

"No, and you'll see they'll let him alone. They won't pick any quarrel with *him*. Every one knows that he goes armed whenever he leaves the house. He always has."

"Well, I'm glad I'm not in his shoes, anyway," said Will, with his hand on the door knob. "And if I's you I'd keep out of the way of that MacBean crowd for *one* while."

"We'll see about that," said Hubert. "I'm a free-born American. I haven't committed any crime; and neither have any of my friends that I know of. And it doesn't agree with me to be ordered about by people of that stamp. Now, good night, Will, I'm lame and sore from head to foot, and I'm going to bed."

The following morning Hubert spent over the pages of Cæsar's Commentaries—making up some arrears of translation in anticipation of Mr. Brewster's return next day. His cuts and bruises were rapidly healing, though he still limped from the effects of a vicious kick on his leg, and when he put on his hat had to find a new position for it on his head to avoid a painful swelling. Early in the afternoon he came down the front stairs with a cricket bat in his hand and started for the street.

"Oh! where are you going?" cried Will, who had followed him into the hall.

"To Mr. Windom's," answered Hubert, steadily.

Will stopped short, his mouth wide open with astonishment.

"*Jee-rusalem!*" he whispered. "They'll kill you sure. They *mean* it. Do you know I heard some men saying out on State Street this morning that Mr. Windom is a spy and ought to be hung?"

Hubert made no reply, but opened the door, and, with the bat under his arm, passed out into the street.

## CHAPTER IV

### MOB LAW

THIS time it was Margaret who opened the door in response to Hubert's knock. On seeing him she seemed to have some question on the point of her tongue, but to think better of it before the asking. She led him into the library and went to call her father; and in the interval before Mr. Windom's appearance Hubert had leisure to examine the room and its furnishings more completely than ever before.

The first objects to attract his attention were two Revolutionary muskets that lay on a table in the corner near the door. It would seem that these might be preserved as interesting relics of the struggle in the preceding generation; but Hubert, who was very familiar with firearms, noted almost at once that their flints were in perfect order and that there was powder in their priming pans. From these indications he concluded that they were loaded and ready for use. He had not seen them before, and doubted whether they had been in the room on the preceding day.

Turning to stand before the fireplace and warm his hands at the blaze, he saw on the mantel above a pair of naval pistols, brass mounted, of elegant workmanship, and with heavy barrels nearly ten inches long. These likewise had fresh powder in their pans. And Hubert was certain that they were not on the mantel at the time of his previous visit.

He was puzzling over these things when a door from a rear hallway opened and Mr. Windom entered. The merchant's manner gave evidence of unusual agitation; and he began speaking before Hubert could utter any greeting.

"Master Delaroche, I am much afraid it is not safe for you to be here. I learned this morning that some of the low-class people in the town are accusing me of communicating with the British—of preventing the escape of Decatur's ships by signaling with the blue lights that were seen. I had nothing to do with them; but now I recall that I did say yesterday to an acquaintance on State Street that Decatur showed good judgment in turning about as he did. That remark has doubtless been twisted and magnified by rumor, and with some other expressions of mine in the past, has brought this accusation down on me."

"What did you hear this morning?" asked Hubert.

"Oh, a friend of mine took me aside and warned me that there was violent talk going about—talk of tar and feathers, of gallows, ropes and what not. And as I came up from the wharf a gang of young rowdies came after me with stones, so that I was obliged to draw my pistols to frighten them away. Have you heard anything of this business?"

"Yes, I have heard of it. And I have myself been threatened if I came near your place."

"Why, then, do you do so?"

"Because I do not choose to be ordered about in that way. And because I wished to hear your side of the story before I came to any conclusion."

"Well, sir!" exclaimed the merchant, "that shows a fine spirit, I must say; and I thoroughly appreciate your attitude. At the same time it exposes you to needless risk; and I very much wish you had not ventured. I have ordered horses and a carriage which will be here in an hour; and Margaret and I will take ourselves out of harm's way for the time. And now, if you will allow me to conduct you out by the back way and through the stables, you can doubtless get away unseen. That will surely be best under the circumstances."

Hubert stopped for a moment to consider. The situation was really worse than he had realized; and common sense told him it was best to take his host's advice. At the same time he felt a great reluctance to desert his friends in the hour of their peril. The state of mind of the townspeople being what it was, the Windoms' carriage might be attacked on the streets or even stopped by a barricade. With these thoughts in mind, he was beginning to reply when Margaret came running into the room.

"Oh, Father!" she cried, "see all those men coming up the street. What are they going to do?"

Mr. Windom sprang to one of the front windows

and Hubert to another. In the middle of the road was a disorderly crew of fifteen or twenty men. Perhaps half of them had guns or pistols; the rest carried axes, clubs or crowbars. At their head marched brawny Jonas White, the blacksmith.

Windom rushed to the corner of the room and snatched up one of the muskets. Returning to the window, he flung it wide open. By this time the mob was pouring into the yard, and Jonas White was already on the lowest of the steps leading to the front door.

"What do you want here?" shouted the merchant, leveling his gun at the ringleader's face.

White, whose weapon was a sledge hammer, paused in the act of mounting the stair. His followers fell back hastily and took cover behind trees and fences.

"We want *you*," answered White loudly. "Come along now peaceable; and we won't hurt anybody else."

"Get off my property, you low-down scoundrel," said Windom, speaking now in low and level tones. "If you don't, and quickly too, I'll send a bullet through you."

At this the blacksmith hastily retreated; but as soon as he was safely sheltered behind a garden wall some of his followers opened fire on the house. Their aim was poor, for no one was hit by the first volley, though the glass in the windows at which Hubert and the merchant were standing was shattered to bits.

Windom instantly replied with his musket; and one of the more venturesome of the rioters, whose head and shoulders had been plainly visible where he stood behind the garden wall, fell forward with a groan.

"Margaret!" shouted her father, "run to the cellar, quick, and you too, Delaroche."

Margaret ran from the room; but just then another bullet came through the window and struck Windom in the arm, whirling him about and almost felling him to the floor. With an oath he snatched up the other musket, and crouching down behind the window sill, proceeded to use it as a breastwork by extending the barrel over the ledge.

Scarcely knowing what he did, Hubert seized the two pistols from the mantel. There was a crash from the direction of the dining room; and the youth, rushing toward the sound, saw that three of the rioters with axes and bars had mounted to a small veranda on that side and were breaking a way through the French windows. He fired point-blank at the foremost, and saw him fall backward and lie still. Then, shouting threats of a like fate at the others, he drove them from the veranda and back to the garden wall.

Returning to the library he found that Windom still lay behind his breastwork, alert to repel any further assaults. But Margaret had returned to the room and was screaming that the barns were all on fire. Evidently some of the raiders had put a torch to the hay stored there. These buildings were but forty feet from the house, and connected with it by sheds and ells. The flames would be all around them in a quarter of an hour. Already the air of the library was thick with smoke that came in through the shattered windows of the dining room.

"Come, then! Let's to the cellars," said Windom, springing up from the floor and seizing his daughter by the arm. "There may be a chance that way."

Pushing Margaret before him, he rushed into the hallway and down the cellar stairs at the rear. Hubert followed, glancing warily behind to see whether they were pursued.

In the half darkness of the basement they stumbled over piles of bricks and boards and hurried through one dim passage after another. Knowing well that the house would soon be all ablaze, Hubert could see no use in seeking a hiding place beneath it; but he soon found that Windom had realized that also and was proceeding on a totally different plan.

Presently they came to a stop before a little wooden door at the end of a long ell that projected from the main body of the house for sixty feet or more. The bolt and hinges were heavily rusted from long disuse; but Windom loosened them cautiously and opened the panel. Then it became evident that the door was partly concealed on the outer side by a row of lilac bushes.

By this time the barns were blazing up like great torches, the connecting sheds were all afire, and a momentary veering of the wind filled the garden before them with thick, black smoke.

"Now!" cried the merchant, "follow me."

Leaping through the shrubbery, he emerged on the

33

open garden with Hubert and Margaret running hand in hand close behind him.

Then another blast of wind swept the air around them clear of smoke; and they heard the yells of besiegers who had caught sight of them. A musket roared, and Windom fell on his knees, clutching madly at a wound in his breast.

"Go on! Go on!" he shouted when Hubert would have paused to raise him. "Run for your lives. I'm done for."

Hubert grasped Margaret's hand again and raced with her across the remaining open space toward a hedgerow at the rear. A stout fellow with an axe in his hand stepped out from cover and called to them to stop. Hubert aimed his remaining pistol full in his face, and the man leaped aside. Gladly withholding his fire, Hubert, with his terrified companion, crashed through the hedge and into a nursery of young evergreen trees beyond.

Running through these in turn, they found themselves in a coppice of young oaks, where the trees had been cut three or four years before and where the sprouts, now ten feet tall and covered with half-dried leaves, afforded perfect concealment. Here they dodged and doubled about for three or four minutes to confuse any who might be following; then emerged into a larger wood where they could run more swiftly.

Soon they were on a little rise in the woodland whence they could plainly see the blazing house, now a quarter of a mile away. Scarcely pausing for an instant, they hurried on through the woods and rocky and hilly pastures in a southwesterly direction for two or three hours. Then, emerging on a hilltop, they saw before them the blue waters of an inlet and of the sound beyond.

A road ran along the foot of the hill, but no persons or vehicles were in sight upon it. Half a mile to the right were two white-painted cottages. Directly in front of the fugitives, and two hundreds yards from shore, lay a beautiful, three-masted schooner, swinging at her anchor ropes in the outgoing tide.

# CHAPTER V

## CAP'N BARNSTABLE

THE wintry twilight was already descending, but Hubert could make out a number of figures, moving rapidly about on the deck of the vessel. Shouted orders floated across the water, men swayed at ropes and spars; and the lad, who was already familiar with many seafaring activities, knew at once that preparations were being made for sailing. Then the vessel's stern swung round till, even in the gathering dusk, the watchers could read the name *Blue-bird* in large black letters just below the taffrail.

Hubert started forward with an eager cry. A plan had flashed upon his mind by which they might accomplish their escape. He knew Captain Barnstable, the skipper of the *Bluebird;* at least, he had met him once when the old sea dog, who was visiting friends at Carrington, had given a talk on the West Indies at a schoolhouse gathering. And only the week before, Hubert had caught sight of him on the New London docks, though at that time he had not ventured to accost him. Now the boy suddenly became convinced that if he and Margaret could once get aboard the schooner they could

36

take passage for wherever she was bound, and would be safe from any pursuers.

After hurriedly explaining his plan to his companion, Hubert seized her hand and ran with her down the rough hillside to the road. Thence a half-overgrown path led through the salt grass and over a crazy plank footway to a little wooden jetty that formed the nearest approach to the schooner's anchorage.

Standing on the pierhead, Hubert shouted and hallooed for two or three minutes together, waving his cap to the men on the schooner and indicating by violent gestures his request that they send a boat ashore. It was all to no purpose; the men merely glanced at him and went on with their work. Even when Margaret joined her cries to his in a long, high-pitched scream, the fugitives attracted no more notice from the busy mariners than would a pair of wailing sea gulls.

Half frantic with the thought of this fast-waning opportunity, Hubert glanced about for some more effective means for getting his message to the vessel's commander; and his eyes fell on a leaky skiff that was chained and padlocked to the end of the pier. It contained a pair of oars and a battered tin bucket that had evidently been used for bailing. There was no time for picking and choosing. Seeing that the craft floated in spite of three or four inches of water in the bottom, Hubert determined to employ it if he could possibly get it free from its moorings.

Leaping into the boat, he swiftly examined the ring

through which the chain was passed; but this was securely bolted to the bow and could not be detached without proper tools and the expenditure of time and care. Climbing on the pier again, he seized on the padlock to decide whether it could be broken. It was a stout and well-made product of a country locksmith, but breaking it open seemed the only chance for getting the boat free, so Hubert brought two large stones from the shore, and, placing one of these under the chain, made Margaret hold the lock edgewise upon it. Then, swinging the other stone in both hands, he proceeded to use it as a hammer. But after half a dozen blows he was obliged to give over this attempt, as he seemed to make no impression on the iron, and there was serious danger of wounding Margaret's hands. At last the girl herself made the needed suggestion:

"See the staple there," she cried. "Can't we pry that out somehow?"

The staple which fastened the chain to the pierhead was also of good wrought iron and stout enough to resist any strain that would ordinarily be brought to bear upon it. But in an instant a plan arose in Hubert's mind for loosening it. In the bottom of the boat was a round iron bar, an inch or so in diameter and perhaps a foot long, which for some purpose had been sharpened at one end like a spike. Thrusting this through the staple, the boy lifted on the free end with all his might. The prongs were deeply set in the oak planking and refused to stir. Then he took one of the oars, inserted the handle beneath the round iron, and, seizing the shaft halfway down to the blade, lifted again with his full strength. This double leverage was too much for the rusted fastening; the staple groaningly yielded and soon was free from the planking. Then, after assisting Margaret to a seat on the rear thwart, handing her the bucket and telling her to bail for her life, Hubert threw the oars into their sockets and rowed swiftly toward the schooner.

At the rail, as the boat approached, stood a stout, oldish man in rough, seaman's clothes and sou'wester hat and with an angry frown on his face.

"What do ye want?" he yelled.

"I must come aboard and see Captain Barnstable," answered Hubert.

"Oh! Cap'n's busy. Too busy to be botherin' with *you.* Can't you see we're *sailin'?*"

With this, the mate turned contemptuously away and began talking to some of the seamen behind him. But Hubert was not to be rebuffed by any authority save that of the last resort. He had a voice of such strength and carrying power as to have gained for him the nickname of "Trumpet" among his playfellows at New London. In this extremity he made full use of it.

"I tell you I have to see Captain Barnstable," he shouted in tones to wake the dead.

This mighty hail produced the intended effect. Men on the schooner's deck dropped their work to gaze in astonishment; the mate returned with an angrier face than before; but the door of the cabin opened, and the skipper himself came to the rail. Gray-bearded, with keen blue eyes and rosy countenance, broad and stooping shoulders and great, powerful hands, the captain was a picture of competence and authority. It was evident at a glance that he was one who would tolerate no trifling.

"What do ye want?" he demanded, as fiercely as had the mate.

"I am Hubert Delaroche," was the reply, "son of Squire Delaroche of Cedricswold. I met you a year ago at Carrington."

"I don'no nothin' 'bout that," returned the captain, sourly. "I can't remember every boy I see. What do ye want *now?* We're in a hurry."

"We want to come aboard first. I have something to tell you personally. It's a serious matter."

"Wal then, come on if ye must," growled the skipper. "Tie up here to the waist, and be quick about it. We're losin' time and tide."

A moment later Hubert and Margaret were sitting in the captain's cabin, on one side of the table, while the old seaman sat leaning his elbows on the other. Without wasting any words, Hubert told him of the charge lodged against Lucas Windom by the gossips of New London, the attack on his house, the killing of two of the rioters and finally of Windom's death in the garden when they attempted their escape. Margaret sobbed desperately as the recital proceeded, but the captain sat gazing steadily into Hubert's face, his eyes giving no hint at all of either belief or disbelief. Just as the story was completed they heard the anchor hauled over the rail and deposited with resounding noise on the forward deck.

"So this young gal here is Lucas Windom's darter," said the captain at length.

"Yes, sir," answered Margaret, drying her eyes meanwhile with her kerchief.

"And where did you 'spect to go?"

"I don't know," began Margaret, beginning to sob afresh. "We . . ."

"We hoped you'd take us somewhere—anywhere," put in Hubert, "to get us away from here."

"I don'no 'bout that, young man. You say you killed some of them folks. Kind of like helpin' the enemy myself, ain't it?"

"No, it isn't, not a bit. Mr. Windom never had anything to do with those blue lights."

"I ain't so sure 'bout that. I've heerd of him. He was a Peace Party man, I guess, and his father in Boston was a Tory in the old days. Maybe he didn't tell you all he did."

"My father never did any wrong," sobbed Margaret. "He was the best father any one ever had. And now they've *killed* him."

"Wal! Wal!" said the captain quickly. "You ain't to blame, anyway, I guess. Your mother livin'?"

"No, she died two years ago."

41

"Wal! that *is* kind of too bad, I vow. Leaves you all alone, don't it?"

"Yes. We hadn't any one in New London. And my aunt in Boston never liked us; and she quarreled with my father long ago. I wouldn't go near her."

Happening to glance through the cabin window just then, Hubert saw the shores slowly moving as the vessel drifted with the tide that was running toward the sound.

"Oh, captain!" he exclaimed, starting up and looking back toward the little pier. "Can't you give me a man in one of your boats, and let me take that boat back that we came out in? I had to borrow it; and if we can't get it back to the pier, I'll have to find some way to pay the owner for it."

"P'raps you'll need it to go back in yourself. *I* ain't said you could go with me, you know."

"No, but I'm very sure you're going to."

"Wal," said the captain. "We'll see 'bout it. I ain't helpin' any *spies,* not if I know it."

Opening the cabin door, he shouted some orders to the mate, then went on up the ladder to the deck. Five minutes later he returned to the cabin. Margaret was still sobbing at intervals; and Hubert's mind was wretchedly divided between hope and fear.

"I guess you're an honest boy after all," said the captain, as he reseated himself, "or you wouldn't be worryin' 'bout that boat at a time like this. I guess you've told things 'bout as they are. I've sent the boat

42

back. 'Tain't really dark enough yet for us to resk it in the Sound. But now what are you goin' to do? I'm goin' to Norfolk, in Virginia, if I manage to git past the Britishers."

"We'll be glad to go to Norfolk, if you'll allow us."

"Mebbe we can fix it," said the captain, slowly. "I got a little room that I fixed up for my own darter two years ago; but sence the war come on I ain't wanted her, nor her mother either, aboard here at all. There's too much resk—what with the blockaders and all. The young lady might have that, I s'pose."

"As for you, young man," he went on after a moment. " 'Less you want to go into the foc's'le, you'll have to use the little bunk here't the cabin boy (when I had one) used to sleep on. S'pose you can put up with that?"

"I'll put up with anything whatever to get out of this neighborhood and get Margaret to some safe place. The farther away from New London the better."

For a minute or two the captain sat looking out of the window toward the darkening shore. At last he said, slowly:

"Wal, I guess you got the right idea of it. Course she's got to be looked after. I don'no what can be done, but I'll help ye what I can. And now I see them fellers comin' back from carryin' your boat ashore. It's goin' to be a good dark night, jest as I figgered it would be. And if we have any luck at all, we'll slip

43

past them Britishers out there jest like a gray cat in a fog."

So saying, the skipper stepped briskly from the cabin, and Margaret and Hubert shortly heard his lusty voice on the deck. Very soon the darkening shores of the inlet began to slide swiftly astern as the schooner gathered headway.

The clouds hung low overhead and the night rapidly closed around them, but no lights appeared anywhere on the vessel. As they came out on the waters of the Sound all noises were hushed and necessary orders were given in undertones. Hubert, who was straining his eyes from the forward deck, saw nothing of the British cruisers.

Next morning it was evident that wind and tide and old Dame Fortune had all alike been favorable, for when the fugitives ventured out on the sloping deck in the midst of a fine northwest wind and a choppy, white-capped sea, no enemy sail was in sight, and blue water was everywhere around them.

# CHAPTER VI

## BLUE WATER

THERE followed several fair and breezy days during which no sail of any sort was sighted and Hubert had enough and more than enough of time for reflection. At every moment when his mind was not occupied with something immediately before him vivid memory pictures arose of the scenes in the burning house, the shooting down of the rioters, Windom's tragic end and the mad flight through the evergreens. For his own share in the conflict the lad had no feeling of guilt. He had aided in resisting the lawless invasion of a household wherein he was a guest; and, with the traditions of his race as to the right of any citizen to freedom from such invasion coloring all his thought, he could only wish that this resistance had been more successful. Still he thought with a shudder of the victim of Windom's musket as his crumpled body lay across the garden wall, and hoped most ardently that the man who had fallen before his own pistol shot had not been mortally wounded.

For diversion from these gloomy thoughts Hubert keenly studied the activities about him, and in a short time had vastly increased his knowledge of the sea and

45

of the ways of those who followed it. He sat on the after deck with Margaret, who, in these new and vivid surroundings had now recovered the appearance at least of cheerfulness, and noted every detail of the management of ropes and sails and steering gear. Or he followed Peleg Johnson, the surly old mate, from one task to another, narrowly watched his motions, and tried his patience with constant questioning.

On the sixth day, when the schooner was perhaps a hundred miles from Cape May, an event occurred which was to make the knowledge thus gained of practical importance. The upper works of a brig were sighted on the eastern horizon, and Captain Barnstable, not knowing whether the strange vessel was an enemy, crowded on all sail in an attempt to leave her astern. This effort proved vain, for though the schooner was fast and most skillfully handled, the brig turned out to be faster still. After an hour or so of sailing under all possible canvas it became evident that the smaller craft would soon be overhauled. The roar of a gun from the brig and the ricocheting of a solid shot along the wave tops left no doubt of the stranger's intentions. Sundown was yet two hours away, and there was no sign of a protecting fog in which the schooner might have been maneuvered out of reach. Wholly unarmed as his vessel was, Captain Barnstable had no choice but to yield; so, with bitter groans at his ill fortune, he hove to and ran up the American flag.

What then was the joy of those aboard the schooner

IT BECAME EVIDENT THAT THE SMALLER CRAFT WOULD BE SOON
OVERHAULED.

when the brig answered this by the display of the same bright ensign! They had anticipated capture, with all its attendant miseries; but now their formidable pursuer seemed a friend and protector. The brig commander ran close to leeward, nevertheless, and signaled that he would send a boat aboard.

Even before the officer and his men had come up the ladder which was lowered for them, the captain of the *Bluebird* had satisfied himself as to the character of his visitors. The brig was a privateer out of Baltimore; and her captain doubtless intended to be certain before releasing the schooner that her registry was that which she claimed.

A piratical-looking boat's crew, armed with pistols and cutlasses and led by a villainous, red-nosed mate, came over the rail. They were courteously greeted by Captain Barnstable and his first officer, who had the ship's papers in his hands ready for inspection. The privateersman gave but a cursory reading to these; then led his men to the hold to inspect the cargo. After five minutes or so the party returned to the deck, four of them carrying a small cask of New England rum which had evidently been seized as contraband.

While watching the lowering and stowing of this prize in the longboat, Hubert made a discovery which he hastened to communicate to Captain Barnstable. A tarpaulin had been thrown down in the bow, and protruding from under the edge of this were two pairs of seamen's boots. It was clear that some members of the *Bluebird's* crew were deserting, and hoped to get aboard the privateer unseen.

When the captain heard Hubert's story, instead of hastening to the rail, he went forward and scanned the remainder of his crew where they were assembled on the deck. Having thus made sure of the identity of the deserters, he surprised his informant by saying:

"Let 'em go. Don't say a word now. Let 'em think they've fooled us."

With Hubert he stood at the rail as the privateers pushed off, looking, with a derisive grin on his face, at the feet of the deserters that protruded so ridiculously from under the tarpaulin.

"Let 'em go," he said again when the boat had covered half the distance to the brig. "That's the cook, Mulatter Jim, and that feller, Thorpe, from Liverpool. They made trouble for me all last v'yge—stirrin' up trouble 'mong the men 'bout every namable thing, till I was near ready to clap 'em in irons. And now they think they've come it on me by gittin' away and jinin' that privateer where there'll be no handlin' of cargo and such a lot of prize money. Wal, I know what it is on a privateer. I v'yged and fit on one of 'em for three years durin' the old war. And they can have all they want of it. It's kind of like piratin' anyway."

"Won't it leave us short-handed?" asked Hubert.

"Yes, it will—some. Though I guess we can manage if it don't come on to blow."

Margaret, who had heard part of this conversation

50

from the cabin door, came aft just then and joined them at the taffrail.

"I tell you," cried Hubert, "let me work 'fore the mast for the rest of the voyage. I believe I can help."

"Why, no doubt you can, boy!" returned Captain Barnstable, heartily. "You ain't be'n like a landsman any time. I'll tell the mate. He thinks you're a smart one, reely, though he *does* growl at ye like a dog sometimes. Have ye ever b'en aloft?"

"Many a time—in the *harbor*."

"Wal, it'll be some different here. Howsomever, you be careful, and you can try it. We got only eight men now, and that reely ain't enough."

"And I can help too," put in Margaret, eagerly. "I can cook. I know I can cook better than that yellow man."

"Can ye now?" said the captain, slapping his leg and laughing hugely. "Wal, you shall try it. Mebbe we'll git on *better* stid o' *wuss* on 'count o' them desertions."

It proved to be even so. Margaret was installed in the galley, and Hubert went to work with a will under the old mate's orders. Next day all hands voted the meals better than before; and Mate Johnson was already hugely proud of his apt pupil in seamanship.

Two days later it "came on to blow" as the captain had feared. For twenty-four hours the sea was swept by a midwinter gale; the captain and mate went aloft with the rest to handle sail like common seamen; and no one save the steersman was relieved for a watch below. Hubert performed every task given him with the spirit of a soldier in a desperate campaign; and never knew he was tired till the wind had abated and the danger was past.

The next afternoon, in the midst of bright sunlight and a gently rolling sea, Captain Barnstable and Hubert were enjoying a well-earned rest on the after deck. Margaret was busy in the galley and old Mate Johnson was forward, overseeing some repairs to the pumps. The events of the past few days had greatly contributed to the friendship between the captain and his young companion; and now for half an hour Hubert had been retelling the tale of the blue lights and the subsequent happenings in New London. He was still firmly convinced of the innocence of Lucas Windom; and in his defense had advanced many of the arguments the ill-fated merchant had made against the whole conduct of the war and in favor of an early negotiated peace.

Captain Barnstable listened without comment during the lad's eager recital; but when it was done replied, slowly:

"Wal, I guess he had the right of it in *some* ways. The' ain't no doubt at all that we b'en gittin' the wust of it in all the fightin' on the *land;* and now our fightin' ships are all locked up in the harbors, jest as he said they was. But as for Napoleon Bonyparte, he ain't the wust tyrant th' ever was by any *means*. The common men in France come nearer to havin' their rights right

52

*now* than they ever did before.  I guess he *is* ambitious
and dangerous to the other nations in Europe; but it
looks to me as if his power was broken for good by
that war he made in Rooshy where they say he lost a
million men.  And I tell *you*, the danger we got to look
out for here in America ain't from France but from
*England*.  Do you know what old Ben Franklin said
'bout it not long before he died?"

"No, did he talk about this war?"

"Yes, *sir*, he did.  He said 't we'd fought one war
with England—the Revolutionary War—to git our in-
dependence, but that we'd have to fight another one to
*keep* it."

"Did he say that?"

"Yes, he did.  And he was *right*.  Wise old thinker
he was, too, as we ever had.  I've thought of it lots of
times and seen jest this a comin'.  It ain't the plain,
common men in England that's plannin' to conquer us.
I've known lots of 'em, and they're good men.  They
want to live and let live.  It's the Tories and 'ristocrats,
jest the same as 'twas in '76.  Jest as soon as they git
into power in the gov'ment they begin to plan the same
as King George the Third and old Lord North.  Why!
what Mr. Windom told you 'bout the British holdin'
Canada and the west, and hemmin' us in is right.
That's what they mean to do.  And when they git us
down fur enough they'll offer us peace on the basis of
bein' British colonies again."

"Oh! do you believe they'd go as far as that?"

"Why! I surely do. I've had a British officer tell me, right here on my own deck, not five years ago, when I was protestin' 'ginst his takin' my seamen, 'What do *we* care where they were born? Your whole country is only a lot of rebel colonies!' "

"Do you think they have any chance to get us down like that?"

"Wal, I don'no. We warn't prepared at all, didn't have no well-drilled army, and we've had some *awful* blunderin'. . . . That's why all our campaigns have turned out the way they have. The British have be'n kep' too busy in Europe to take advantage of it the way they might have. But you watch now and see if the next big move they make ain't to git control of the Mississippi. There's New *Orleens*. We're holdin' it by a mighty slender thread, and they know it. You'll hear of a great big fleet and army goin' up the river, takin' possession of the city and then workin' northwards. And if our folks don't wake up in time and do somethin' big to stop it, why we're beat, that's all."

"Is it true that the men they took off our ships were deserters from the British navy?"

"It's true that it *begun* that way. We had lots of British deserters on our ships; and seein' the treatment their officers give 'em, I don't wonder *at* it. But they warn't content with that for long—no *sir*. They'd simply come on board, pick out any good likely fellers they see, and take 'em along. They took six off my vessel one day—that's the time the leftenant told me that about the rebel colonies—and four of them fellers was born in Massachusetts. I'd known 'em all their lives. And it left me so short-handed that when it come on to blow, as it did next day, and a whole lot wuss than yistiddy, we come terrible near to bein' capsized and sunk. Yes, *sir*, I know somethin' 'bout the impressment of seamen—p'raps full as much as Lucas Windom did."

Just then the lookout at the masthead called out lustily: "Land on the starboard bow!" and the captain rose and went below to fetch his glass. Soon Hubert could make out a misty shore line which the mate informed him must be Cape Henry.

By great good fortune none of the British blockaders were in sight. The wind was brisk and fair; and Captain Barnstable, making the most of his opportunity, set all sail and passed through Hampton Roads in the early hours of a moonlit evening. Before midnight they were safely anchored within sight of the docks at Norfolk.

# CHAPTER VII

## MUSTER CAMP

THE next afternoon, while all hands were busy unloading the bales of woolen cloth that formed the greater portion of the cargo, Captain Barnstable returned from the town, accompanied by a middle-aged and prosperous looking gentleman, and for half an hour was closeted with him in the cabin. When the visitor had gone the captain called for Hubert, and motioned him to a seat on the opposite side of the table.

"I don'no quite what we're goin' to do 'bout the gal here," began the old mariner, anxiously. "I had in mind to go up to Cap'n Blaisdell's plantation—that's up the river a piece—and see if I couldn't git him and Mrs. Blaisdell to look after her. They're nice folks, and I think they'd do it if I was to ask 'em. But now here comes Mr. Blanchard—him that was here jest now—and he wants that I should unload jest's quick's I can and then take on a cargo he's got for Martinique. They kind of think the Britishers'll be away from out here for a day or two more. And if so, I can git out and away. He's got 'bout forty niggers he'll put on to the loadin' job first thing in the morning. And I've got to be right here to see to things."

56

"Why don't you write a letter to Captain Blaisdell," asked Hubert, "and let me take it to him?"

The captain heaved a sigh of relief.

"Wal, now, that's jest what I was thinkin' of. And I'm glad you're willin' to undertake it. I *ought* to go myself, I know; but as things be, I don't see how I can."

"Of course you can't," agreed Hubert. "We've been trouble enough already."

"No, you ain't be'n no trouble at all. You be'n a *help*, both of you. And I'd willingly spend a couple of days gittin' this thing settled if Blanchard hadn't come in the way he has. Wal, I'll write a letter to Blaisdell that I guess'll fix it all right; and you'n Margaret can go up there to-morrer. It's 'bout fifteen mile up the river. I'll send Tom Bisbee to row with you and to bring the boat back. I guess the two of you can pull up there, takin' it with the tide, in mebbe four—five hours."

This seemed to Hubert a perfectly reasonable arrangement; and Margaret, when she was called in and the situation explained to her, took the same view of it. As soon as she understood she was to leave the vessel the next morning she declared that she must get to work in the galley and in her own room, so as to leave them in order. Soon the captain was hard at work on his letter. Hubert meanwhile took the opportunity to write to his parents at Cedricswold, briefly recounting the happenings at New London that had

57

made him a fugitive, the events of the voyage on the *Bluebird* and his errand for the morrow at the Blaisdell plantation. He had time to complete and seal his missive and to go ashore and mail it at the post office before Captain Barnstable, who worked somewhat laboriously with a fierce grip on his pen and with his tongue protruding at the corner of his mouth, had come to "Your Most Obedent Servant" at the end of two exceedingly black and inky pages. When at last he had affixed his bold and unmistakable signature the letter was given to Hubert's keeping.

In the morning, after bidding somewhat sorrowful good-bys to Captain Barnstable, Mate Johnson and the rest, Hubert and Margaret set off in the ship's boat up the river. The Blaisdell landing was reached at noon; and, as the tide had just turned, Tom Bisbee made haste to land his passengers and to head back toward the ship.

The two young peopie made their way up a long cart road toward the great white mansion which, with its green-blinded windows and columned portico, was visible through the bare branches of closely surrounding trees.

Half a dozen foxhounds rushed out from kennels in the orchard, and disputed the visitors' way until they were dispersed by some negro field hands who came from the group of small, whitewashed buildings at the rear of the mansion. On the broad front veranda a more hospitable greeting awaited the travelers, for as

soon as the black house-boy had carried within
Hubert's message that he had a letter to Captain Blaisdell from Captain Barnstable of the *Bluebird,* a tall and
beautiful lady, with large black eyes and soft, silvery
gray hair, came into the hallway and, announcing herself as Mrs. Blaisdell, ushered them into the great
sitting room beyond.

Hubert introduced his companion and himself, and
handed Mrs. Blaisdell the captain's letter. But upon
reading the address, she said at once:

"Why! I'm very sorry, Master Delaroche, but Captain Blaisdell is away from home. He's with his company at Muster Camp, 'way back in the Blue Ridge. I
hardly know when he will be home again."

Hubert was somewhat dismayed at this ill chance, but
after a moment's thought, he said:

"Then won't *you* read the letter, ma'am? I know
what it contains, and I'm sure that's what Captain Barnstable would wish."

After seeing her guests comfortably seated, Mrs.
Blaisdell complied. On reaching the end, she looked up
at her guests with a most winning smile and said,
slowly:

"You are very welcome, both of you, to Blaisdell
Plantation. I can surely say that much, although, in the
captain's absence, I should not feel justified in making
any definite reply to Captain Barnstable's proposal.
That must await my husband's decision. You see how
it is, I'm sure."

"Yes, ma'am," replied Hubert.

"I would hope to make myself useful," said Margaret. "I can cook and sew."

"My dear child!" exclaimed Mrs. Blaisdell, "I hope that that will not be necessary. And I know very well that our old Aunt Jerusha would never allow you or any one else to work in her kitchen. Please regard yourselves as our guests, both of you, for the time; and we will see what Captain Blaisdell thinks as to the rest of it when we can hear from him."

Gladly enough the young couple acquiesced in this arrangement, and they spent some happy days as the guests of the gentle Mrs. Blaisdell. They took long rides about the country, sometimes accompanied by their hostess or her daughters and sometimes alone together; and Margaret began to emerge from the melancholy which had enshrouded her since her father's death. Maidie and Susan seized upon her at once as a wonderful playmate; and it soon developed that she could teach them the French language, an accomplishment which their mother was very anxious for them to acquire.

After four or five days, however, during which Hubert had time to get well rested and to explore pretty thoroughly the plantation and the immediate neighborhood, he became decidedly uneasy in spite of his pleasant surroundings. He had found no way of being useful and began to think of himself as one who presumed on the hospitality of chance acquaintances.

Gradually a plan grew up in his mind; and on the sixth day, after discussing it with Margaret, he put it before his hostess.

"I've been thinking, Mrs. Blaisdell, that I might perhaps borrow one of your horses and ride to the Muster Camp to see the captain."

"Ride to the Muster Camp! Why! It's near two hundred miles."

"I know; but I could cover it in five or six days, riding the colt I had yesterday."

"Do you think you could find the way?"

"Oh, yes. I have a tongue to ask questions with; and I've made several long journeys in that way."

"And you'd just as soon go all that way alone?"

"Yes, ma'am. The only thing that would worry me would be lest some harm should come to your horse. If 'twere my own, 'twould be different."

"Oh, as to that, I'm sure you'd look after him as if he were your own. And I know from watching you yesterday that you're a good rider."

"Yes, ma'am, I've done a great deal of riding."

"Very well, then. I know you must be getting restless here. And it's true that the captain may not return for months. His company was called out, you know, for possible service against the Indians after that terrible battle at Fort Mims; but now it seems we're not to send any troops over the mountains. There was some talk of their being mustered out, but nothing certain; and there might be some new emergency."

"I'll bring you all the news when I return," said Hubert, happily.

"That will be most welcome," answered Mrs. Blaisdell, smiling in sympathy with his enthusiasm. "For it must be admitted that the captain is a poor letter writer. He writes me once a week, to be sure; but his letters are all of drilling and hunting; and we learn nothing of what they are to do. Perhaps you *can* do somewhat in that way for us."

So on the following morning Hubert made ready for a journey which he estimated might occupy a fortnight. The young black horse, known on the plantation as "the colt" was to be his mount, and the rider was duly equipped with storm coat and blanket roll from Captain Blaisdell's ample store. His plan was to see the captain at the camp, secure his approval for Margaret's stay at the plantation, then, after returning with the news of this decision and with the borrowed horse, to make other arrangements for himself. The nature of these was still very vague in his mind; but he was sure that it would not be safe for him to return to New England for a year or so, or, indeed, until the end of the war. He had some thought of the navy and of a midshipman's berth; but for the most part was content to postpone any definite planning until Margaret's immediate future was secured.

He still had one of the pistols which had figured in the defense of the Windom house; and Captain Barnstable had made him a parting gift of the excellent sailor's knife he had used on board the *Bluebird*. With these weapons he would have been content; but when all good-bys had been said, and he was already mounted, Mrs. Blaisdell came hurrying from the house with a short-barreled rifle which her husband had used for fox and coon hunting and which Hubert had greatly admired.

"Here!" she cried. "Take this for better protection on the roads. In these days you might meet with bad men; and the mere sight of this may be something. I would be sorry indeed if any harm befell you."

Hubert was so overcome with gratitude that he could hardly express his thanks. The house-boy came close behind his mistress, bearing powderhorn and bullet pouch; and in much confusion Hubert hung them from his shoulders. Farewells were said again; and, noting a telltale moisture in Margaret's eyes, Hubert spurred away somewhat hastily at last. From a hilltop a quarter of a mile away he turned to wave once more and saw his gallant hostess with Margaret and the two younger girls by her side, on the lawn by the manor house, and all with waving kerchiefs in their hands. It was a pretty picture indeed, and one that was to remain long in his memory.

Six days later the young messenger rode into Muster Camp, only to find it deserted and forlorn. Not a soldier was to be seen, and no smoke arose from the stick-and-clay chimneys of the huts that had housed

63

them. At first Hubert could find no one in the neighborhood who could give him other news of thc militiamen than that which he had heard immediately on the outskirts of the camp ground—that they had been paid off and discharged three days before; but at last he found the keeper of a little store who knew Captain Blaisdell, and was able to tell him something of his whereabouts.

It seemed that neither the captain nor the majority of the members of his troop—the Dominion Mounted Rangers—had been in sympathy with the order which dispersed the Virginia militia as soon as it was learned that Kentucky and Tennessee had forces in the field to cope with the Creek uprising. They had come into camp expecting to be led against the savages who had perpetrated the horrible massacre at Fort Mims, and they were not disposed to accept three months of camp life as a substitute. The result was that Captain Blaisdell had called for volunteers to follow him through the Cumberland Gap to the westward and offer their services to the Tennessee governor at Knoxville; and seventy-six out of the eighty members of the company had come forward.

Three days since they had ridden away toward the mountain pass, and might by this time be traversing the Tennessee uplands. They had set no time for their probable return, as this depended entirely on the fortunes of the campaign. The storekeeper was postmaster as well, and remembered a letter which had been

dispatched by the captain to Mrs. Blaisdell at the plantation.

In this juncture Hubert gave but little time to deciding on his future course. Here was a new obstacle;
and an obstacle was *a thing to be surmounted.* Stopping only to rest and feed his mount, to send a brief
note to Mrs. Blaisdell and Margaret, and to gather from
the storekeeper all possible information as to the route,
he set forth on the trail of the Rangers. By nightfall
he had traversed some of the lower passes of the Blue
Ridge, and, in a tangle of hills and streams beyond,
was for the first time on this journey obliged to make
camp in the forest.

With the aid of his sheath knife, he soon had built a
wall of evergreen boughs that would shelter his back
from the north wind, and in half an hour had collected
wood for a roaring camp fire. The weather was mild
for January, and but little snow was on the ground.
By great good fortune a fine, plump rabbit paused only
forty yards away to gaze in wonder at the flames, and
Hubert knocked him over with a rifle bullet.

When the meat had been dressed and was roasting
over the embers he had no regret that he had not
encountered here another back-country inn such as
those in which he had spent the past three or four
nights. Such an acceptable addition was the rabbit
meat to the drier fare he had brought in his haversack
that he determined to keep a sharp watch on the
remainder of his ride for game of any sort, and to

65

live like an Indian off the country he traversed. Twice during the afternoon he had noted where deer had crossed the trail but a few hours before, and now the prospects seemed excellent for bringing one down on the morrow.

Lying on a bed of dry leaves and pine needles, with these thoughts in mind, amid the odors of the forest and the sounds of the wind in the branches, he sank by slow degrees into the deepest and most refreshing sleep he had known since he left New London.

# CHAPTER VIII

## ON THE CUMBERLAND TRAIL

NEXT morning Hubert was early astir. By the time the sun made its appearance over the tops of the hills he had traversed on the preceding day his breakfast was cooked and eaten, his pack remade, and he was riding down the western slope. All day he kept a sharp lookout for game; but he killed nothing larger than a turkey, for although he crossed several fresh deer tracks, it did not seem best to leave the trail to follow them. He halted for a noon-day rest in a little upland valley where the trees were so scattered as not to shade out the grass and where therefore the colt found ample grazing. Another such glade, with a clear, mountain brook running down its center, was his camp ground for the night. Two days later he rode through Cumberland Gap and found himself in the beautiful hill country of the Tennessee and Kentucky border.

Within ten miles of the pass the young adventurer came to a parting of the road where the wider and more traveled pathway led straight on toward the southwest in the direction of Knoxville and another and narrower one veered off to the right toward the Kentucky mountains. From the information he had had from the storekeeper at Muster Camp the first was plainly the road which should be traversed by the Rangers; but it was the right-hand path that showed the marks of the recent passing of a numerous company of horsemen. After dismounting and examing both trails for a hundred feet or more from the junction, Hubert decided that the company he was following had turned to the right, and that his only course was to do likewise. The hoof marks were not fresh; and it was evident that some time had elapsed since the riders passed this way, so Hubert had no immediate hope of overtaking them. Half an hour later he came upon a settler's cabin, and there learned that the Rangers had ridden by two days before. Also that the campaign against the Creeks had been abandoned, and that the Tennessee volunteers were returning to their homes.

Knowing that the company was encumbered with pack animals which would need wider and smoother trails than a lone rider like himself, Hubert eagerly inquired if there were not some practicable short cut by which he could gain some of the distance by which the horsemen were leading him. In reply the mountaineer told of a bypath that led off the main trail to the left, under a lightning-struck pine two hours' ride farther on and rejoined it on the other side of a long range of hills.

"It's ten mile o' purty tough travelin'," he said, "and kind of a blind trail, too, ef you ain't used to it; but ef

ALL DAY HE KEPT A SHARP LOOKOUT FOR GAME.

you stick to it, and don't git lost nowheres, you'll save mebbe twenty-five mile—most a hull day o'ridin'."

This was good news, so, thanking the settler for his information, and declining a well-meant invitation to " 'light and stay the night," Hubert spurred eagerly forward, determined to traverse the short cut and regain the main trail before dark.

By three o'clock he had come to the lightning-blasted tree and made out the faint pathway that led to the westward.  For a mile or two it was easy enough to follow; but after that it commenced ascending a succession of sharp slopes among thick woods of locust and thorn and huge, jutting ledges.  Presently the rider reached a place where the recent heavy rains had erased nearly every trace of the pathway, and where he was obliged to dismount and lead his horse for a mile or more and many a time to pause and choose between three or four possible directions.

The afternoon was cloudy, and it was now rapidly growing dark in the woods; but Hubert, having determined not to make camp until he had emerged on the main trail, pushed on determinedly.  It was soon evident, however, that his course in choosing this byway had been much more energetic than wise, for when he had left the summit of the rise behind him he was obliged to admit to himself that he had utterly lost his way.  The path he had been following seemed first to have divided into a half dozen still fainter trails and then to have disappeared altogether.

Hubert was thinking of the little pocket compass that had been a birthday gift from his mother and ardently wishing that it had not been left at the Brewsters' in New London, when a sight met his eyes which caused him to draw rein suddenly and to forget everything else in the world.

On a fallen log, straight ahead, and not forty paces away, was a huge black bear. The creature had already sighted him and stood calmly watching, his little, black eyes shining beadlike in the dusk. The colt was equally aware of the vicinity of a dreaded enemy, and stood stock-still, trembling and snorting and with feet planted wide apart. A shot from horseback under such circumstances is a very risky thing; but Headlong Hugh, from the moment he sighted the big beast, had but one thought—he must bring him down forthwith and make good his character of hunter and woodsman. Throwing his rifle to his shoulder, he took quick aim at a point just between the gleaming eyes and fired.

At that instant the young horse leaped aside, wheeled around and bolted along the way he had come. Hubert was flung on his hands and knees on the ground, his rifle falling six feet away. Scrambling to his feet he was just in time to see the furious rush of the great beast that had evidently been wounded and was now charging upon him, open-mouthed.

The young hunter turned and fled for his life through the open woodland, expecting every instant to be overhauled and seized. A hundred feet away was a ledge some ten feet high, with a young locust tree growing out of a cleft about four feet from the ground. Making a frenzied leap, Hubert clutched the stem of this sapling, and, with a speed which was astonishing even to himself, scrambled up to the top of the ledge.

There he had a moment's respite, for the bear ran completely around the rock in search of an easier ascent, and failed to find any, for the other faces were even higher and steeper than that upon which the young tree grew. But presently the great beast, with his head bleeding from the wound where Hubert's bullet had glanced off his skull, came back to the place where the boy had climbed up, and proceeded to follow him.

For a moment Hubert thought that his last day had come, for it was evident that the bear was an able climber and would soon be upon him. Then, in the nick of time, he remembered the pistol that he carried at his belt. Snatching it out, he looked to the priming, only to find that there was no powder in the pan, and that the weapon would almost certainly miss fire. Working faster than ever in his life, he pulled the plug from his powder horn and emptied half a spoonful of the grains into and all around the priming pan. Already the great, black head of the beast was visible over the angle of the ledge. In another moment he would draw himself over. Hubert rushed forward and thrust the muzzle of his weapon within a foot of the gleaming jaws. The bear's mouth flew wide open, and he gave utterance to a frightful roar of rage. With a desperate lunge,

Hubert pushed the pistol barrel fairly into the great, red cavity and pulled the trigger.

At once the bear's body, that by this time was half way over the edge, wilted down as though struck by a lightning bolt, and, sliding from the rock, became a crumpled heap on the ground below. The bullet had pierced his brain, and after the briefest struggle the great beast lay still. Hubert stood on hands and knees on the edge of the rock for half a minute, peering at his victim and making sure that he had himself come through unscathed. Then he leaped down, ran and regained his rifle, and looked about for his horse.

A moment's scanning of the rapidly darkening valley served to show that his mount had deserted him. This was a misfortune indeed, and, barely remembering to recharge his rifle, Hubert started away on the trail, hoping to overtake the animal in some thicket near by. But by this time it had become so dark that the youth had not proceeded forty rods before he had utterly lost the traces of the horse's flight and nearly all sense of direction as well. With some difficulty he retraced his steps to the ledge where lay the carcass of the bear, and there sat down to reflect on his situation.

His horse was gone and with him his blanket roll and provisions. He was utterly lost in the woods, and must depend on making his way on the morrow by the position of the sun, if indeed the day were not so cloudy as to make that impracticable. Lacking a mount it was very unlikely that he would be able to overtake the

74

company, even if he found the trail again. And if he did so, how could he account to Captain Blaisdell for the horse and the other property that had been loaned him. The remembrance of Mrs. Blaisdell's kindness was like a whiplash on a bare back. Was he really much better than a thief? In a passion of self-contempt in which he could have kicked himself Hubert remembered the nickname his father had bestowed on him, and for the first time realized how well it fitted him.

Still, as he remembered after five minutes' dejected musing, he had all his weapons and ammunition, and the means of making a fire. Before him lay the bear's carcass; and this surely ought to provide him with food for the time being. It was very late in the day; and Hubert, who had not paused for any mid-day meal, was all at once aware of a raging hunger. Guided by what little light still came through the branches, he set to work with might and main to skin the animal and to cut out the haunches. This done he gathered dry wood by the light of the moon that now appeared over the eastern hilltops, and soon had a cheerful fire. A tripod of green stakes was quickly erected, and a haunch of the bear meat suspended from it. In half an hour the roast was done to a turn, and although it was somewhat lean and tough by reason of the winter season, Hubert found his meal perfectly satisfying.

When he had eaten his fill, he began making preparations for the night. The moon now brightly lighted the glade, and he made out one great ledge on the hillside of which the brow overhung the base so far as to form a protection from rain or snow, and, on two sides at least, from any prowling enemies. In the hollow was an accumulation of wind-blown leaves that could be made to serve as mattress and coverlet.

In a short time Hubert accumulated a goodly pile of wood, including some thick and heavy chunks from an old stump, and moved his camp fire to the new location. When he had the fire well started in front of the ledge he piled upon it some of the heaviest of his wood, carefully cleared the ground between it and his bed of grass and leaves and sat down to rest and to plan his course for the morrow.

An hour later, after again replenishing his fire and seeing that it did not threaten the material of his couch, he drew over his feet and legs a thick covering of the damp leaves, buttoned his storm coat up to his chin, stretched out at full length under the sheltering ledge, and soon was sound asleep.

When he opened his eyes again it was dawn in the forest, the fire had burned down to coals and a tall young Indian, in deerskin blanket and feather head-dress, sat ten feet away, with a long rifle across his knees.

## CHAPTER IX

### BLUE FEATHER

HUBERT sprang up and grasped his rifle. The Indian, however, only waved his hand in friendly fashion and said, in surprisingly good English:

"Don't worry. I am not your enemy."

"Who are you?" demanded Hubert, still dazed with the suddenness of his awakening, "and what do you want?"

"I am Blue Feather, the hunter," was the reply. "Have you any red pepper?"

"No," replied Hubert, slowly. "But how do you come here? I thought all your people had left these woods."

"That is a long story," said the Indian, whom Hubert now perceived to be a youth but little older than himself. "And you—are you lost in the mountains here? You have no horse or blankets."

"No, for I lost them last night, just after I reached this place."

And Hubert went on to tell briefly the events that led up to his present plight.

"Huh!" was the young Indian's response. "You should not have fired at a bear while riding a young

77

horse like that. No wonder he ran and threw you. And now what will you do?"

"Well, I'm first going to cook and eat some break-fast. Then I'll see what I *can* do. Will you eat some bear's meat with me?"

"Huh!" said the Indian again, "I have eaten this morning, but that was two hours ago, and, as you ask me, I will eat again with you. You must have more wood for the fire."

Rising, he laid his gun against a stone and started down into the valley to break some of the dry branches from a fallen sycamore. Hubert, watching him intent-ly, saw that his dress was a strange combination of savage and civilized garments. The Indian wore a pair of woolen trousers with deerskin shirt and moccasins like those of the white backwoodsmen, but the blanket that was fastened around his shoulders in place of an overcoat, the necklace of bears' claws and headdress of blue jays' wings were such as his ancestors had doubt-less worn long before the coming of the white men. Strangely enough, all his clothing was clean, and the gun he had just laid down was well cared for and showed none of the rust and dirt that usually encrusted firearms of Indian ownership. Then, too, the young brave's speech was nearly as correct as Hubert's own, showing no trace of Indian dialect and but little of that of the white settlers of the region. Altogether he was a most unaccountable person; and Hubert's mind, while he bathed his face and hands at the brook and sliced and broiled the meat over the rekindled fire, was so busy with these puzzling circumstances that he totally forgot his own immediate problems.

Blue Feather likewise thoroughly washed both hands and face before seating himself near the fire and accepting the broiled meat which Hubert handed him on a sharpened twig. From a pocket he produced a small metal box containing salt, and, opening it, handed it with some ceremony to his host. Across the mind of the young white traveler came the recollection of what he had read somewhere of the Arabs—that any one with whom they partook of bread and salt became by that token a friend and ally; and he wondered greatly whether the same custom was observed among the American Indians.

In any event the salt was a most welcome addition to the broiled meat; and very soon both the youths were eating with eager, morning appetites. No words were spoken while the meal was in progress; but as soon as it was finished Blue Feather rose and said:

"The next for you then is to find your horse and blankets."

"Yes," replied Hubert eagerly. "Do you think there's any chance of doing that?"

"Oh, we will find him," answered the Indian with a smile. "We have only to trail him far enough. But maybe we will find him dead—that is, his bones—if the wolves have found him. Come then and we will see."

Catching up his gun, Blue Feather started toward the trail of the colt which he had already remarked upon during his journeys after fuel. Hubert seized his rifle and his few other effects and followed close behind. The tracks in the earth and leaves, which Blue Feather seemed to note as readily as a beaten pathway, led down the glen for a quarter of a mile, then along the bank of a larger stream in the valley beyond.

Blue Feather traveled at a slow dog trot, varied occasionally by a loping gait where there were bushes underfoot. For the first half hour the white boy easily kept pace, for the second he managed by desperate efforts to keep the Indian in sight, but when they had covered ten miles or more and Blue Feather showed no sign of slackening, Hubert was obliged to call out for a halt while he regained his breath.

The Indian seated himself on a log and looked with a grim smile at his companion, who lay full length on the forest floor, panting like an overridden horse. After five minutes of resting Hubert rose to his feet, and they were off again as before. Blue Feather now carried his deerskin blanket on his arm, and grasping his rifle by the middle in his other hand, ran as easily as if on a half-mile jaunt and wholly unencumbered. Tall, lithe and straight-limbed, and slender at the waist, he was the picture of a runner. He was handsome, too, with his strong and regular features and bright black eyes; and his figure brought to Hubert's mind, as he followed him through the forest openings,

the thought of the bearer of tidings of the victory at
Marathon.

So, alternating between running and resting, they
traversed hill and dale, waded brooks and skirted sedgy
marshes for another hour or more. Then, on the border
of a grassy meadow, Blue Feather suddenly raised his
hand for a halt and pointed toward a clump of beeches
on the other side. At first Hubert could discern
nothing through the dry leaves that still clung to the
branches, but presently made out the figure of the colt
where he lay on the ground.

At the same moment the poor strayed animal perceived his master and sprang up and uttered a long
whinny of greeting. The lads crossed the meadow on
the run, leaping like squirrels from one wild-grass tus-
sock to another; and Hubert was overjoyed at finding
his mount unharmed. Saddle and bridle were still in
place, though deeply scratched by the forest boughs,
and the pack and blanket roll lay just as he had fastened
them on the preceding morning.

It seemed that Blue Feather's camp was not more
than five or six miles away, and soon the two youths
were on their way thither. Hubert had offered his
companion the opportunity to ride and lead the way;
but the Indian lad had scornfully refused, saying, what
could not be denied, that Hubert was far more tired
than he was. Any offers of payment for his services
he likewise refused; and Hubert, realizing that his new
companion had taken a liking to him and was serving

without prospect of reward, did not pursue the matter at the time, but determined to be on the watch for opportunities to even the score.

Coming over a little hillock in a grove of honey locusts, with the light wind in their faces, they startled a buck and doe that had been feeding among the rushes in the glade beyond. Blue Feather was in the lead, and he now threw his rifle to his shoulder with a lightning-like movement, and when the stag turned at right angles among the trees on the farther rise, brought him down with a shot through the body. Hubert cheered loudly at this success, leaped down from the saddle, ran forward and performed a dance of triumph all round the quarry. And the young Indian, though saying never a word and scrupulously avoiding any hint of boasting, was evidently not ill pleased with this demonstration of his ready marksmanship.

The deer was lifted to the horse's back and lashed in place; and they went forward again in single file. Blue Feather now held the bridle rein and followed Hubert who walked a dozen paces ahead, with his rifle at "Ready," and with his mind aflame with the thought of sighting more big game. None was seen, however, and in another half hour they came out into a tiny, grass-grown clearing in the midst of which stood a hunter's cabin of poles and clay.

Blue Feather hastened to tie the horse to a sapling, then opened the cabin door and stood aside for his guest to enter. Within the place was of surprising neatness;

the earth floor had been cleanly swept with the broom of twigs that stood in the corner; blankets were straightly folded, and the few cooking utensils hung in order on the walls. The fireplace and the whole of one end of the lodge were of rough stone and the other walls of heavy poles, cleverly notched and fitted at the corners. Clay plaster made the walls weather-tight, and the roof had been freshly thatched with marsh grass and flags. Blue Feather briefly explained that he had come upon this deserted cabin several months before, spent a week in repairing it, and had since made it his home. He was of the opinion that it had been built ten years before by one of the sons of Daniel Boone.

While Hubert built the fire and brought fresh water from the brook, Blue Feather was dressing the carcass of the buck. In an hour the meat was roasted, the corn bread was browned on the griddle, and the two lads prepared for a woodland feast. Blue Feather even had a small tin of coffee, which he now produced as for a notable occasion; and this, adding its fragrance to that of the roasted venison, furnished the last-needed suggestion of a backwoods holiday.

They lingered long over their meat and drink, experiencing the keen delight of all healthy mortals in rest and food after strenuous labor. Afterward, as they sat in deep content before the fire, Hubert told his companion much more fully than before the events which had driven him from New London, his experiences at sea, and the object of his journey to the Muster

Camp and into the Kentucky wilderness. The young Indian was keenly interested, especially in the account of the voyage—for he had never seen the ocean—and asked many questions with regard to Lucas Windom and Margaret and the old sea captain. When these had been fully answered both were silent for a time, while they gazed at the glowing coals in the fireplace and listened to the wintry wind in the sycamore branches. At last Blue Feather said gravely:

"You have told me, Hubert, the story of yourself. And now, if you wish to hear it, I will tell you in turn what has happened to me since I can remember, and how I come to be here, wearing the clothes of a white man, living in a house that one has built and speaking his language."

"I am very glad if you will tell me," replied Hubert. "I have been wishing to ask you since I first saw you."

"Well, then, the first that I remember I was in a village of my people, the Shawnees, far to the west of here and on the other side of the river they call Ohio. I played and hunted and fished with the other boys of the tribe and knew nothing of any other way of living. When I was perhaps ten years old our men went on the warpath against the white men; and one day they returned with many scalps. They had surprised a little log fort in the woods, and killed all the people within it. Another party of our braves came in soon after, that had killed many deer and buffalo. Some brought a keg of liquor also that had belonged to a trader whom

they had killed; and a feast began that lasted for three
whole days. Then, at night, when half our men lay
helpless with the rum, a war party of white men suddenly burst in upon us and began killing all who stood
in their way and setting fire to the wigwams. There
was fierce fighting all around me, and soon all our men
who were not drunken had been killed or driven into the
forest, and many women also, for they too fought with
tomahawks and knives. And when I saw my father
shot down beside me I seized a long-handled ax that was
ours and ran at a tall white man who was coming
toward us with a smoking gun in his hands. I meant
to kill him, but he was too strong and quick for me. He
knocked the ax from my hands with the barrel of his
gun; then, never striking me, pinioned my arms and
fastened them with his belt.

"That man was Captain Harriman from the Smoke
Ridge country in Virginia. He took me home with
him, and though I was like a young wild beast he finally
made me see that he meant well by me and would do
for me more than my own father ever could have done.

"He sent me to school in the village there; and his
wife grew jealous of me because I learned faster than
her children. I was in the school five years, and the
master planned to make of me a learned man and to
show what an Indian could do who had right teaching.
But Captain Harriman was not rich, and he needed my
help in his sawmill; so in the times when I was not in
school I learned that work. Three years ago my

schooling stopped, and I spent all my time in the mill except for a day now and then when I would go to the woods to hunt or fish, sometimes with Captain Harriman and sometimes alone. The woods, after all, seemed my home, and I never could bear to be long away from them.

"But in a year Captain Harriman died of a fever; and in another his widow had taken a new husband. This man was named Barrett. He was a tall, thin man, with sharp, little eyes; and he thought of nothing but getting money. He brought two black men to work in the mill, and often stood over them with a whip when they did not move fast enough to please him. It was not long before I could see he thought of me in the same way as the black men. I was to work and work and do nothing else; and now my food was apt to be only that which the family did not want, and my only bed was the shavings in the mill.

"But he never ventured to strike me with his whip until one day I came from the house with my fishing lines and started for the woods. He ran in front of me then and said:

" 'Go to your work there. You can't be running off like this.'

" 'No,' I said. 'I am not your negro. I have worked many days, and now I go to fish.'

"At that he started forward and struck me with his whip. Well I remember how the lash curled 'round my body. But he struck only once, for I seized the whip

86

from his hands and struck him on the head with the heavy handle. He fell down in the path; and his wife came screaming from the house, cursing me for a murderer. I went back to the house, took my gun and other things and came away. As I went down the path toward the woods I could see that Barrett was sitting up on the ground while his wife was binding a wet cloth about his head. Meanwhile the saws had stopped, and the black men were peering out from the mill with grinning faces.

"I came over the Blue Ridge to the mountains here; and since then have lived the life of a hunter. Two or three times in a year I go to Knoxville to sell my furs and to buy powder and other things which I cannot get in the forest. But I have no wish to remain in a town, even for a night. My people are of the woods, and so am I."

When Blue Feather's tale was finished and Hubert's further questions answered, the short wintry afternoon was nearly half spent; but the youths found time for a circuit of his trap line, which had been neglected in the morning.

Returning to the clearing, they took off the pelt of a beaver that had been found in one of the traps, and hung it with the deerskin on the end of a long slender limb, that when released sprung up fifteen feet from the ground and out of the reach of wolves and bears. Then they spent the hour that remained before dark in shooting at marks, such as beech leaves pinned with thorns to tree trunks or an egg-sized stone swinging as a pendulum at the end of a twenty-foot line. And Hubert gained the respect of his new companion by nearly equaling his marksmanship.

In the evening Blue Feather invited Hubert to become his partner in the winter's hunting, offering to share equally the proceeds of all the pelts they secured, including those he had already taken. This offer was extremely attractive to Hubert, for he had already conceived a strong liking for the Indian lad and for the life he led. But he explained that it was impossible to accept it because of his unfulfilled errand with regard to Margaret, and because he still had in his possession Captain Blaisdell's horse and other gear.

Blue Feather could not dispute the rightness of this decision, but he nevertheless remained unwilling to give up the plan he had proposed. The result was that he offered to accompany Hubert to the camp of the Rangers and await the outcome of the interview with Captain Blaisdell.

# CHAPTER X

## OLD HICKORY

AT daybreak the boys were astir, and before an hour had passed their breakfast had been cooked and eaten and all preparations made for their journey. Blue Feather now believed that he knew the destination of the Rangers when they turned aside from the Knoxville road and into the hill country northwest of the gap. He recalled a camp in the Thorn River Valley which had been built by a large party of Virginia hunters two years before. They had left in good condition half a dozen pole cabins and a long open shed for horses. Very likely their party had included some who were now members of the Ranger troop; and it might well be that Captain Blaisdell had decided to spend some time in hunting in that region of abundant game. In that way they could rest and refresh their horses in the meadows near by and lay in a stock of provisions in the form of dried and salted meat.

Thorn River Valley was twenty miles away; but Blue Feather, well knowing the country between, counted on reaching it in eight or nine hours. Then, he said, if they found no one there, they could remain for the night and set out next morning for some other likely halting place.

At four in the afternoon they sighted the station from a hilltop half a mile away; and Hubert caught his breath at the loveliness of the scene. The cabins stood in an open grove of sycamore and sugar trees, on a little eminence in the midst of a wide, grassy valley. Thorn River, here only five or six paces wide, foamed and glistened among the rocks of its channel in the center of the intervale, and, to the west and north, stretched an endless series of blue and rolling hills. Far-seen, deep-forested valleys showed tints of rose and purple in the sloping sun rays; and billowy, snow-drift clouds sailed miles overhead in an azure sky. Here at last, he told himself, was a country as beautiful as anything he had seen in the valley of the Connecticut.

Nearer approach showed that the camp was indeed occupied by the Rangers. Presently the travelers were challenged by a sentry, and, at Hubert's demand, were taken immediately to Captain Blaisdell. The captain, a tall and handsome, black-eyed man of late middle age, was sitting at a table before one of the cabins, studying what appeared to be a rough map of the surrounding country. Half a dozen of the Rangers were lolling in the vicinity, smoking and talking, while a larger number were engaged in building additional shelters in the grove near by. The newcomers learned, however, from the talk of some of the groups they passed, that more than half the men of the company were away on hunting expeditions.

Captain Blaisdell instantly recognized the horse

which Hubert was leading, and seemed to look on the lads as they advanced with some measure of suspicion. But this was quickly dispelled when Hubert introduced himself and his companion and presented Mrs. Blaisdell's letter. The captain bent his brows on this for a moment; then interrupted his reading to bid the visitors be seated on the bench near by and to tell one of the Rangers to take the horse to the shed at the rear.

When he had finished reading the letter he turned to Hubert with a number of questions, and drew forth a brief but sufficiently explanatory account of his and Margaret's adventures. At the tale's conclusion the captain sat for a little time tapping his boot with a riding whip, which had lain on the table, while Hubert and Blue Feather awaited his decision. Just then one of the Rangers came running up the slope from the trail, calling out:

"Oh, Captain! There's a man here you'll want to talk to. He's got some news for us."

The captain rose at once, and all turned to look at a horseman who was now ascending the knoll, fifty yards behind his announcer. He was a tall and lank backwoodsman, roughly dressed in the fashion of the region, and carrying a long rifle across his saddlebow. His mount was lean and rough-coated; his blankets, in the roll behind the saddle, were worn and faded; and the rider's whole appearance, with his brush-torn frontier hat and untrimmed hair and beard, was that of one who had traveled hard and far. Yet there was in his manner and in the level look of his keen blue eyes a measure of dignity and authority, and he dismounted and came forward to acknowledge Captain Blaisdell's greeting with the easy air of an acknowledged equal.

"I'm Cap'n John Harkness," he said, "jest back from Gin'ral Andrew Jackson's expedition, down on the Coosa."

"And I am Captain Blaisdell of this troop of Rangers here," was the response. "I am happy to meet you, Captain. No doubt you can tell us some news."

"You better b'lieve I *can*," said the Tennesseean. "That's jest what I come here for. The' was a feller named Anderson come into Knoxville day before yist'dy. And he said 't he was with you a spell on the Cumberland Trail, and 't you'd turned off up in here to hunt and rest up your horses."

"That's true."

"And was you intendin', Cap'n Blaisdell, to come down and help us 'ginst the Creeks? Or the Redsticks, as they call 'em?"

"Yes, that *was* our idea. But we'd heard, just after we came through the gap, that the campaign was all over for this winter; and we didn't know really whether we'd go on to Knoxville or not."

"Wal now, I'll tell yer," said the backwoodsman earnestly. "It *ain't* over for this winter. Or if it is, it's the worst setback this country's had sence the Revolution times. And if we set down and let it be as it is, them murderin' Injuns 'll break out wuss'n ever

92

inside o' three months. They're gittin' all the arms and powder they want from the Britishers. It's a cryin' *shame*. Old Hickory marched off last fall, when the call come, when he had a wound that oughter kep' him in bed for two months more anyway. He's managed and drove and fought like a very devil to give the Red-sticks the beatin' they need. He's beat 'em, too, where-ever he could come up on 'em—that is, the smaller bands—and he was all fixed to go after Weatherford and the main body of 'em, right in their dens and fast-nesses, when his army all went to pieces—the men claimin' their enlistments had run out an' that they warn't clothed and fixed for winter campaignin'.

"Governor Blount he's stood back o' the gin'ral all he could; but he did give in at last 'bout the enlistments; so one regiment after another's gone and left him. And now Gin'ral Jackson's down there in the woods at Fort Strother with I don't believe more'n a hundred and fifty men. Why! The Redsticks could take the place if they realized it, and kill and scalp everybody there, like they did at Fort Mims."

By this time all the men in the camp were crowded around the speaker and their own leader, who faced each other across the little table.

"Why! What made the men act so?" demanded Blaisdell. "Didn't they go down there just purpose to kill off that murdering crew?"

"Yes—yes, they did—and, far's *fightin'* goes, they did well enough in the two-three actions we had. But

93

Old Hickory, he never knows what *wait* means when he gits started on a thing like this. They *didn't* have overcoats and blankets enough for winter campaignin', and then, wuss still, we had the awfulest times gittin' the provisions through. We had to cut our own roads, you know, and jest about make our own wagons. And the contractors that was going to bring down meal and beef and so on, they had trouble gittin' down the Tennessee to Fort Deposit, 'count o' the water bein' so low, and they jest *didn't* git through with half enough. We couldn't hunt much either. That'd be jest what the Redsticks wanted—to git us out in the woods in small bands where they could ambush us. The whole army'd ben on half rations for weeks, and there was a lot of sick and wounded and so on. Twice they picked up and started for home in a body. And Old Hickory stood in their way with a loaded rifle in his hands and not more'n half a dozen of us to back him up, and he swore he'd shoot the first man to cross a certain line. And both times he stopped 'em so—jest out er clear grit and determination. But at last came Governor Blount's word that the enlistments reely had run out, and he couldn't hold 'em any longer.

Old Hickory he says to me, 'Harkness,' he says, 'you go on back to Knoxville. Gin'ral Coffee's goin' to Nashville to do all he can to stir up volunteers; an' you go and do likewise at Knoxville. By the Eternal!' he says, 'we *got* to beat these murderin' savages if we're goin' to have any peace in our homes right in Tennessee. An' if we give up now, all the friendlies 'mong the redskins that've stood by us so fur will grab up their arms 'n go'n join the Redsticks. An' then we *will* have a war on our hands. The next thing that'll happen'll be a British expedition up the river to New Orleans. And when we're fightin' the Redcoats on one side an' the Creeks on the other, then we'll see somethin' o' the times I used to see in Carolina when I was a boy. Them folks in Washington better wake up pretty soon or we jest *won't have* any United States for 'em to pre-side over.' Yes, sir, that's what he said."

"And so they all came away and left him."

"Yes, sir, that's what they did. It was the most shameful thing I ever see. Talk about half rations! Why! Old Hickory says to me, 'Git me some *men,* Harkness, for God's sake—*men that'll stand to and fight* while there's need of it and not begin to talk about home soon's they git cold or hungry. And I'll stay right here at Fort Strother till they come, if I have to live on roots and acorns.' Yes, sir, that's the kind of man he is. I tell *you* I ain't no cry-baby; and I've seen some purty tough things in my day; but when I come away from that camp the tears was runnin' down my face as they ain't before sence I was a child. There's a *man* for you. We ain't got many like *him.* And somethin's got to be done and done quick, too, if we're goin' to save this country from goin' back to where it was fifty years ago."

When the Tennesseean had finished speaking every

one was silent for a moment. Then Captain Blaisdell looked about at his men and asked, huskily:

"How many of us are here now?"

Several had come up since the messenger appeared and now a hurried count showed a little more than half the company.

"Well!" said the captain, "we'll go into this by and by when they're all here. I want every man to hear what Captain Harkness says. Then we'll see what we'll do. You'll stay with us for the night, Captain. And maybe we can find you some help."

"I b'lieve you will," answered the backwoodsman heartily. "You men come from too good a state to hang back when the's a need like this comes up."

"We'll see. We'll see," responded Blaisdell, with a strong grip of the other's hand. "And now, men, let's get things shipshape. It's just possible we may be moving to-morrow."

In the evening Harkness repeated his plea before the whole company which had been drawn up in double line in the open space between the cabins. At the close of his talk Captain Blaisdell stepped forward and said in a high, clear voice:

"Now, men, we are Virginians; and the fathers of many of us followed Washington from Boston to Yorktown. Are we the kind of men that General Jackson has asked for?"

"Aye! Aye! Yes, we are!" came the answers in swelling chorus.

"Very well, then. Let each man who will volunteer to serve under General Jackson *in the way he has asked* step forward two paces from the line. Forward—march."

At this the whole of both lines went forward and halted in perfect formation, two paces nearer their leader. And now Hubert Delaroche and Blue Feather ran from where they had been standing, a little behind Captain Blaisdell, and planted themselves at the left of the line.

Captain Blaisdell drew a long breath and gazed at the scene before him with glistening eyes. "Men," he said solemnly, "you make me *proud* that I should be the leader of such a company. And I believe you'll continue to make me proud all through whatever it is that awaits us. Now every one get to work and make ready for an early start. We'll ride for Knoxville in the morning. Troop—dismissed."

"Captain!" cried Hubert, who now came running from his place in the line. "I've volunteered—and Blue Feather, too."

The Captain looked confusedly at the two lads who with eager faces confronted him.

"You?" he questioned vaguely. "I'd forgotten all about you. You want to join the troop? Let's see! How old are you?"

"Seventeen, next April," answered Hubert.

"I am nineteen years—as near as I know," said Blue Feather.

"Well, let's see," said the captain. "That won't do. We don't have any one in the troop that's under eighteen."

"But I'm here, and I've *got* to go," answered Hubert, stubbornly.

Captain Blaisdell eyed him for a moment in silence. Then with a sudden gesture of decision, he said:

"I'll tell you, then. You just come in as my aide and messenger. And, as for Blue Feather here, he can be a scout and hunter. Neither one of you need join in regular form; but if you come in that way, you'll understand that you're under orders just as much as if you were enlisted."

"Very well, sir," said Hubert, joyfully. "We agree."

"Yes," said Blue Feather.

"Very well, then. You, Delaroche, may continue to use the horse and arms you have. And we'll make some kind of shift to mount Blue Feather, too. And you wanted to know about that girl you left at the plantation. I haven't given it a thought, but I'll write to Mrs. Blaisdell to-night, telling her to keep the young lady there till we return. Remember now, we'll start early in the morning."

He turned away to answer half a dozen of the Rangers who stood at his elbow with eager questions as to this or that detail of their preparations. The boys found their way to a sleeping place, and soon were wrapped in their blankets and dreaming of the toils, the dangers and the triumphs of forest warfare.

# CHAPTER XI

## DISCIPLINE

B EFORE the sun was over the eastern hills, the Dominion Rangers were on their way toward the Tennessee capital. Hubert rode close behind the two captains, and gained from their discourse of backwoods campaigns and battles much knowledge of the ways of the Indians and the best methods of dealing with them. Blue Feather had departed yet earlier than the company, and was on his way to his cabin, where he meant to assemble his belongings and make ready for an absence that might last for half a year. His traps and cooking irons would be hidden in a cave near by, and the peltries made into a pack to be taken to Knoxville.

On the evening of the second day the troop rode into the town; and the next morning the young Indian joined them. Captain Blaisdell led the whole company to the office of Governor Blount, who, having been apprised of their intentions by Harkness, received them with open arms. Within half an hour all the members of the Ranger troop had been duly enrolled among Tennessee Volunteers, and Captain Blaisdell, with the governor's eager assistance, was making such further arrangements as were necessary for their embodiment in the battalion then being formed.

Captain Harkness was attending similarly to the out-fitting of four companies of recruits whose signatures he had secured before riding northward to the Rangers' camp. And so vigorously were all these preparations pushed that within two weeks the men were fully mounted, armed and equipped, and, after five or six days spent in drill, rode away toward the southern wilderness.

In the interval Hubert had posted a letter to Margaret Windom at the Blaisdell Plantation and another to his father at Cedricswold. Both missives were filled with the patriotic fervor which his recent experiences had roused and with high hopes of a victorious campaign. General Jackson had become his hero beyond all others, and Hubert repeated in the letters some of the ringing tales of his exploits that had been heard from the Rangers and from other admirers in Knoxville. Captain Blaisdell and Blue Feather, too, were glowingly described, and the whole expedition was presented in the light of enthusiasm. Hubert had no doubts as to the high importance of their mission. In the beginning of the letter to his father, and again at the end, he declared that the Creek campaign was bound to be the turning point of the war.

On the very day before the southward march began Hubert received a letter from the Blaisdell Plantation and another from his father which Mrs. Blaisdell had

# DISCIPLINE

forwarded. This had been mailed soon after the receipt of the letter Hubert had sent from Norfolk.

The elder Delaroche had gone to New London as soon as the news of the riot and of Hubert's disappearance had reached him, and had spent a week in the town, endeavoring to satisfy himself as to the causes of the affair and particularly whether Hubert's part in it had been a discreditable one. He wrote briefly and characteristically of his conclusions, and inclosed a sum of money for any immediate needs. In the same envelope was a letter from Will Brewster.

DEAR HUBERT [wrote Will]:

I don't know where you are or what you are doing, but I'm writing this and giving it to your father to mail when he finds out.

The militia company stopped the riot at the Windom place finally. They carried Mr. Windom to the hospital, and he's dying there now. Father went to see him right away and then again yesterday when he heard he couldn't live. Father is awful discouraged about him. He told us about it when he came home, and then asked us not to speak of it any more. Mr. Windom is cursing and swearing against the people in the town here and against the government and religion and everything. Father says it's frightful to hear him. He's known him for years, and never heard anything like it. And when something was said about you, he began to curse and swear worse than ever. Father says that it's best to think that Mr. Windom has been put a little out of his mind by what he's gone through, and really is not responsible for what he says. Anyway, they say he can't live but a few days more.

There are a lot of people here that say he got just what he deserved for lighting those signals, and I've heard some say they were sorry you didn't get the same. And then there are others that say just the opposite. Captain Davis—you remember him, he was in the Revolution—he was talking to your father, and he said that there wasn't any real proof at any time that Mr. Windom had anything to do with those signals, and that whenever a mob started out and took the law into its own hands it was just as likely to be wrong as right. And he said that if he had been a guest in Mr. Windom's house when the mob came there, he'd have acted just the way you did. He's a War Democrat, too.

But just the same, if I were you, I wouldn't come back to New London till the war was over anyway. There are a lot of people—like Rowdy MacBean's gang—who say you ought to be shot. I saw Rowdy on the street yesterday, talking with a soldier; but I crossed over so he didn't notice me.

I hope you're having a good time, wherever you are. You ought to, because I guess you don't have to do Cæsar's Commentaries. I wish Rowdy MacBean were off, fighting the Gauls or somebody like that.

Faithfully yours,

WILL B.

Captain Harkness had received a major's commission and was now in command of the battalion. He was in a fever to rejoin his commander at Fort Strother; but Governor Blount, who had received word of other bodies of volunteers going forward from Nashville to reinforce the pitiable remnant of the earlier expedition at the fort, had given Harkness positive orders to assemble and convoy five hundred head of cattle and a large shipment of flour. Thus a part of the journey was made in the flatboats on the Tennessee; and beyond Fort Deposit, where the supplies were landed, the troopers were compelled to ride at a pace in conformity with that of the lumbering freight wagons on a wilderness road thickly strewn with stumps and stones. With all this three or four weeks were consumed, and the column did not arrive at its destination till nearly the middle of March.

Hubert was riding beside Captain Blaisdell as they approached the camp ground. After all the labor and delay of the journey he was even more eager than he had been at Knoxville to see the army that was to inflict defeat on the savages and the leader whose fame had now eclipsed that of all others on the frontier. Tales and rumors had constantly reached them on their way that made of General Jackson an almost legendary hero, with the gifts of superhuman strength and courage and a marvelous immunity to death. To Hubert, Old Hickory had become a kind of demigod: already he placed him with General Washington and Mad Anthony Wayne. So, as the column came in sight of the log stockade and the huddled cabins of the camp ground, he was looking sharply to right and left and all about for the tall, gaunt figure and the shock of tawny hair he had so often heard described.

Just then they saw a column of infantry that was marching very slowly toward them from the center of the group of buildings, to the melancholy throb of muffled drums. Major Harkness halted his troops, and when he saw that the approaching procession would pass out of the camp grounds by the road on which they stood, gave the necessary orders for drawing his men to one side and forming them in double lines, facing the roadway.

"A funeral, I guess," he said to Captain Blaisdell. "We'll present arms as they go past."

Blaisdell nodded gravely, and turned about to pass the order to his first lieutenant. Then a bend in the pathway on which the approaching regiment was marching disclosed the middle of the line. And there, in an otherwise empty space of fifty paces, appeared a small body of men on whom all eyes were immediately centered.

First came a rank of four soldiers with their rifles at "Ready." Two paces behind them walked a man without weapons, with his eyes bent on the ground and with his hands fastened together behind his back. Immediately following him came another rank of four riflemen with ready weapons. At one side, and nearly abreast of the prisoner, was an officer who marched, sword in hand, scarcely taking his eyes from his charge. Prisoner and guards alike slouched forward as they walked, and wearily dragged their feet to the slow march time.

Captain Blaisdell turned to look at the major, who was watching the scene with painful intentness.

"Punishment?" he asked.

The major nodded, without removing his gaze from the prisoner, who was now nearly in front of them. "Must be," he said.

# DISCIPLINE

The column wheeled to the left and the watchers saw what they had failed to observe before—an open grave in the clearing, two hundred yards away, and just outside the limits of the camp.

Soon the regiment was drawn up on three sides of the space, and the firing squad marched with its prisoner to the grave, which was at the middle point of the fourth or open side of the square. A sergeant stepped forward and bound a cloth over the face of the victim; the squad was aligned twelve paces away and the orders given to aim and fire. In a shattering volley, the rifles rang out, seeming to the overwrought ears of the watchers like the fire of a regiment; and the body of the condemned one sank in a heap to the ground.

Without waiting for the return of the executioners, Major Harkness put his troops in motion, and rode at a trot toward the headquarters building. The next two hours were fully occupied in attending to the many details incident to the arrival. Quarters must be assigned, and officers and men made acquainted with their status in the new regiment of which they were to form a part. Captain Blaisdell kept Hubert exceedingly busy with various errands and commissions; and he had not a moment to think of the grim event he had witnessed or to ask any one for explanations.

In the evening Major Harkness came to Captain Blaisdell's quarters, which Hubert was sharing for the time, and told of the events that had culminated in the execution.

"Gin'ral Jackson," he said, "he's always be'n strong for *discipline*. And he's allus *had* it, too—that is, *nearer* to good discipline in the Tennessee Volunteers than in any other militia regiments in the country—so I be'n told. But through the fall and winter here, 'count o' the lack o' provisions and so on, and 'specially 'cause o' the trouble 'bout enlistments running out, the' got to be a whole lot of confusion, and some officers didn't have much control over their companies.

"Now it seems the same things have be'n breakin' out 'mongst the new troops, too, although they've had plenty to eat and wear, and the's no question at all 'bout their bein' subject to the state authority. The's some pretty bad things happened, I hear, some o' the men as good as tellin' their officers they'd do as they pleased.

"Wal, in the last month or so, the's be'n several arrests and trials for insubordination and mutiny; and two-three times the court martials have condemned the prisoners to death. But when the papers would be brought up to the Gin'ral, he wouldn't sign 'em. No sir, he's let 'em off with some lighter punishment every time. 'After all,' he says, 'it's not as if these men were professional soldiers, that'd lived under discipline for years.' But it got to goin' on from bad to wuss, until just the other day, it seems, Gin'ral Jackson said 't the very next man that was condemned by a court-martial should suffer the penalty.

"Now this man—John Woods was his name—he disobeyed some order his captain give him; and when the captain said 't he'd put him under arrest, he dared him to do it—said 't he'd shoot him if he tried it. Wal, 'course the man had to be arrested; and when they brought him to trial the court-martial sentenced him to death for mutiny. And this time the Gin'ral signed the warrant."

"I'd rather see a hundred men killed in battle," said Captain Blaisdell with a sigh.

"So would I. So would I. I guess I *would*," answered the frontiersman, eagerly. "But discipline in this army, now't we got the enemy to meet, is worth more'n the lives of a *thousand* men. War's a terrible business; and it's got some terrible rules. But the closer they're lived up to the sooner it'll be over and done with. I *hope* the' won't have to be anything more done like what was to-day. But, mark my words, if there *is* need of it, Gin'ral Jackson's the man to give the orders and then to see 'em through."

## CHAPTER XII

## THE HORSESHOE

NEXT morning every one in the camp was in a fever of preparation for the great offensive against the Redsticks. Old Hickory now had several thousand men under his command, and supplies were as plentiful as they were likely to be at any later time. Friendly Indian scouts brought word that the Creeks would try to hold what they called the Hickory Ground, at the junction of the Coosa and Tallapoosa Rivers, a hundred miles to the southward. This was said to be sacred territory among the Indians, the Creeks declaring that no white man ever had or ever could set foot upon it without suffering the wrath of the gods. On this account General Jackson made it his particular objective, well knowing that its occupation would be a crushing blow to the spirit of his savage enemies.

The Coosa was high with the spring freshets, and conditions were favorable to the transportation of supplies and munitions on rafts and flatboats. Very soon the greater part of the army was in motion, and in a few days had arrived at a point halfway to the Hickory Ground. There they constructed another fortified station, and named it Fort Williams. While this work was in progress the Cherokee scouts brought word that the main body of the Redsticks were preparing an impregnable fortress at a place called Tohopeka or the Horseshoe Bend of the Tallapoosa, sixty miles to the eastward.

When this news was received, General Jackson lost no time in putting his troops in motion. Leaving a few hundred men at Fort Williams to maintain his line of communications, he led the remainder straight through the forest toward the Indian rendezvous; and three nights later encamped within five miles of it.

In the meantime many further messages had reached the commander as to the character of the position he intended to attack. Weatherford, the half-breed chief of the Redsticks, had learned much of organized warfare from the British emissaries who had encouraged his enterprise. The encampment he had planned at Emuckfau had, a few months earlier, successfully resisted Jackson's attack with a smaller force; and now it seemed he had so placed and defended his forces as to make it impossible to dislodge them without staggering losses. A bend of the Tallapoosa in the form of a horseshoe, and containing perhaps a hundred acres of heavily wooded ground, had been selected, and its natural advantages for defense heightened by a military work that would have done credit to an experienced commander of civilized armies.

Across the narrowest portion of the peninsula formed by the river bend the trees over a considerable area had been felled and the trunks employed to build a log wall seven or eight feet high. It was pierced with many loopholes for rifle fire; and, to make this more effective, the work was not built in a straight line, but had many angles or salients from which a murderous cross fire could be maintained against attackers. The barrier was in most places too high to be readily scaled; so that if an assaulting force succeeded in reaching its base the defenders would be able to shoot down great numbers of them without themselves being exposed. The river was not fordable on any part of the bend, and to attempt a crossing in the face of rifle fire would surely be disastrous. General Coffee, Jackson's intrepid cavalry leader, and hero of many backwoods battles, declared that, without the aid of heavy artillery to batter down the log fortress, any attack would end in failure.

But now, after months of vexatious and costly delay, Old Hickory had the enemy before him; and he determined to disregard the advice of his lieutenant. Seizing a hillock a hundred yards to the left of the log wall, he mounted upon it the two little brass cannon that had been dragged all these miles through the wilderness, and drew up the main body of his force in front of the fortification, just out of rifle range. Then he sent General Coffee with eight or ten troops of cavalry and the Choctaw and Cherokee scouts, with whom Blue Feather was serving, to make a wide detour, crossing the Tallapoosa at a ford some distance below the Horseshoe and encircling the Indian position by way of the opposite bank. The commander had made up his mind to hazard the entire campaign on the outcome of this day's fighting, and meant, that if a victory were gained, it should be decisive.

The Dominion Rangers with several other cavalry commands were with the main body, in front of the barrier. Their horses had been left in the woods farther back, and the men were serving as infantry. When Captain Blaisdell had suggested to Hubert that he remain behind with the horses Hubert had protested so eagerly that the captain hardly knew what to say. Interruptions in the form of orders from the major and occasions for Hubert's employment as messenger had postponed a decision; and now, on the eve of the attack, the lad was posted near by his leader, his rifle and pistol loaded and primed, his limbs quivering and his pulses pounding with excitement.

When time enough had elapsed to allow General Coffee to occupy his position on the farther bank Jackson ordered the little battery to open fire, and advanced his troops to positions within easy rifle shot of the defenses. The Indians at the portholes in the log wall immediately began firing, and some of their bullets reached their marks. The soldiers, however, being well accustomed to the devices of frontier warfare, instantly threw themselves on the ground and crawled to sheltered positions behind rocks, stumps or trees. From these posts they directed a fusillade at the portholes and at the heads of a few venturesome ones among the savages who were firing over the top of the wall. Doubtless some of these shots were effective, for the Tennesseeans were expert riflemen; but the advantage still remained with the defenders, for the projectiles from the two little cannon were useless against the logs of the wall, and the white soldiers were much less securely protected.

For an hour or more the fighting went on in this manner; then, to those on higher ground, a huge, black cloud of smoke became visible in the direction of the Indian lodges, half a mile or more beyond the barrier, and rifle shots and battle yells were heard. The village of huts near the bend of the river was being attacked. Perhaps Coffee's men had managed to cross the river and were now approaching to attack the log wall in the rear. It was evident that the fear of some such thing had entered the minds of the defenders, for the cannoneers on the hillock reported that considerable numbers of them were leaving the wall and running in the direction of the village.

Just then a messenger came crawling on hands and knees to the rock behind which Major Harkness and Captain Blaisdell were sheltering themselves to say that the General wished their presence at a council he was holding in the woods a short distance to the rear. The two officers started back at once; and Hubert, conceiving his post of duty to be with his captain, abandoned the shelter of a pine stump near by and crawled after them.

Coming to the edge of the standing timber, all three

rose and hurried to where Old Hickory was standing, surrounded already by several of his officers. His long, spare figure seemed of giant height, and his steel-blue eyes gleamed with eagerness. He had thrown his hat on the ground, and, as he gesticulated with his right hand, his left was occupied alternately in rumpling a mass of tawny hair and in brushing it back from his face. At his belt he wore a sword and a pair of long-barreled pistols; but, unlike most of his officers, he carried no rifle.

"The question is, gentlemen," he began, "shall we attack at once, or will it be better to delay? Coffee is making some sort of demonstration that distracts their attention. This may be our opportunity."

"Opportunity to lose a whole lot of good men, getting over that wall," growled a colonel. "We might get *to* it, but can we get *over* it? If those redskins stand to their guns, they can do to us what our people did to the British at Bunker Hill."

"True enough, colonel," assented General Jackson. "It's a mighty strong position. That's why I'm asking the advice of all of you. We have no scaling ladders; the men will have to help each other over; and that means that very many will be killed."

"Their chiefs have stopped any more of 'em leaving the line," reported an officer who had just come from the hillock where the cannon were mounted. We could see 'em driving 'em back to their places."

"They can't git away from this neck o' land, can

113

they?" asked Harkness. "Coffee's on the other bank, ready to shoot 'em down if they try to swim the river or git off in their boats. Can't we jest hold 'em here, and starve 'em out maybe?"

"Oh, I don't like that plan," replied Jackson. "They couldn't get away in the daytime, perhaps; but in the night half of them would slip through our fingers. No, we got to finish them to-day."

While this discussion went on Hubert had been standing with Captain Blaisdell who was in the outer ring of officers and perhaps four or five paces from the General. Through the lad's mind had flashed the remembrance of the games of hare-and-hounds that he had played with his schoolmates in the woods and pastures of Cedricswold. One day he and a companion had climbed to the flat top of a great pasture boulder, some ten feet square and nearly as high, the almost perpendicular sides of which had defeated all previous efforts to scale it, and lying there for half an hour had laughed at all the efforts of the "hounds" to find them. When he remembered the means by which this feat had been accomplished, he plucked at Captain Blaisdell's elbow and began speaking eagerly to him, though in a low voice:

"Couldn't we cut some small trees into lengths ten or twelve feet long, and leave the limbs sticking out five or six inches? Some of the men could carry them up to the wall; and they'd do for scaling ladders."

It so happened that no one else was speaking at the

time; and the firing had slackened for the moment; so a portion of this reached the ears of the General.

"What's that boy saying, Captain Blaisdell?" he demanded sharply.

"Why!" responded the captain, "he's got an idea about scaling ladders. It might work, too. I don't know."

"Well, boy, let's hear it," said the General. "Leave the limbs sticking out, did you say?"

Thus encouraged, Hubert stepped nearer to the center of the group and repeated his suggestion.

"By the Almighty!" exclaimed Old Hickory, "I believe it will work. Plenty of the men have got hatchets. Let's cut a couple hundred of those things. They can push the top ends into the space between the top and second rows of logs, and run up them like squirrels. Yes, gentlemen, I believe it can be done. Get the men to work."

Many of the dismounted troopers were armed with long-handled hatchets in addition to their rifles, and in place of the swords of regularly equipped cavalrymen. Two or three hundred men were soon at work preparing these frontier substitutes for scaling ladders, and fifteen minutes later a corps of pioneers was formed on the edge of the wood. Each of the posts was to be borne by two men; and they were to be surrounded and followed by groups of riflemen. Several hundred other men had gathered heavy branches and other forest débris to throw down in front of the wall and form a sloping approach in the manner of medieval siege warfare. When all was ready the word of command was given, and the whole force went forward with a rush—one regiment of United States Regulars in the lead.

The Indians behind their fortification fired with deadly effect; but the white riflemen, coming to close quarters, killed scores of them at the loopholes. The scaling posts were thrown against the wall in a hundred places, and each of them instantly became the means of ascent for a stream of attackers. In two other places piles of poles and branches, thrown down by hundreds of the soldiers, formed sloping approaches to the top of the barrier; and over these the frontiersmen poured, with savage shouts and yells, and in such numbers as to overbear all opposition.

Behind the wall the Indians fought desperately with clubbed muskets, tomahawks and knives; but this resistance was soon broken down, and all the survivors among the defenders retreated to a tangle of fallen tree tops which had evidently been prepared for just such an emergency. From hundreds of hiding places among these and the thickets beyond they opened a galling fire; and it became evident that the taking of the log wall had by no means ended the battle. Most of the Indians were armed with bows, as well as with guns, and many of the frontiersmen were wounded or killed by arrows when they attempted to rush some tangle of briars and fallen trees after having drawn the rifle fire of its defenders.

# THE HORSESHOE

Now the Tennesseeans advanced from tree to tree, crawling on hands and knees or wriggling forward on their bellies, loading and firing as they went, and often outflanking and shooting down a group of their enemies who, lying behind a rock or a log, were successfully defending themselves against frontal attack.

A way had been broken between two bents of the log wall, and through this General Jackson forced his great white stallion, and came riding into the thick of the fray. Every man in the attacking force was anxious to distinguish himself in the General's eyes; so now the whole line pressed forward recklessly; and a dozen brave troopers fell before the fire of their concealed enemies.

"Keep down there, blast ye!" roared the General from his saddle. "Keep down out of sight till ye can flank 'em."

Just then a bullet struck him in the shoulder, and another wounded his mount; and some of his aides ran toward him, insisting that he obey his own orders. But he waved them aside, and reining his bleeding horse to a position where his body was partially sheltered by a great tree trunk, continued to shout orders and warnings.

So the fight went on for hours, the savages disputing every inch of the ground, but steadily outflanked and crowded back by the frontiersmen, and leaving a score of dead and mortally wounded in every thicket they abandoned. Hubert was still following his captain, crawling on his hands and knees from one shelter to another, and loading and firing as he found opportunity.

Captain Blaisdell had just brought down a painted savage who had been insufficiently protected by a small tree trunk, and was drawing another cartridge from his belt when both he and Hubert caught sight of a terrific mêlée that was in progress in a close thicket forty paces to the left. Caleb Adams, an old, gray-bearded borderer, well-known to the whole expedition as a marvelous rifle shot and a companion of Daniel Boone in earlier days, was fighting three of the Indians with no weapon but his empty gun which he held by the barrel and whirled about his head like a battle-ax. Two of the Creeks had tomahawks, and were trying to gain the rear of their antagonist, while the third was using a rifle in the same manner as the scout, and successfully warding all his blows.

One glance served to apprise the captain of the deadly peril of old Adams' situation. Instantly he sprang up from behind the fallen log which had sheltered him, and, catching his own gun by the barrel, ran with all his might toward the combatants, shouting as he went in the endeavor to distract the savages' attention. Ten feet behind him came Hubert, his rifle likewise empty and grasped by the muzzle end for use as a club.

They were too late by seconds to save the life of the old scout, for when they were still twenty feet away one of the Indians struck him down with a tomahawk.

# THE HORSESHOE

The next moment Captain Blaisdell had killed the hatchet wielder with a blow from his rifle butt, and was rolling over and over among the leaves in a life-and-death struggle with his companion, a tall and sinewy savage in the headdress of a chief.

Hubert meanwhile had attacked the one with the gun, and had had the humiliation of having his weapon knocked from his hands at the first exchange of blows. Then, with his opponent's gun butt already whirling through the air toward his head, he saw and seized his opportunity to overthrow him. Not for nothing all those hot-contested bouts in the wrestling ring! Diving like a wolfhound at his quarry, he seized the Indian's knees and flung his body upwards. The musket harmlessly struck the ground, and its owner, after describing a curve in mid-air, came down with a crash on head and shoulders among the bushes and leaves.

Instantly Hubert sprang upon him; but the Indian was not disabled, and now began a furious struggle to twist the white youth under him or to use the knife that still hung at his waist. He was a tall man and as tough and wiry as a birch withe. Hubert soon found himself well-nigh overmatched. Over and over they rolled, like furious dogs in mortal combat. Now Hubert was above and desperately striving to pinion his powerful antagonist; and now the savage was uppermost and only prevented from using his weapon by Hubert's desperate quickness in twisting from beneath him.

In one of these dizzying turns, when for a second or

two Hubert was astride his enemy, he had a glimpse of a similar battle that was proceeding between Captain Blaisdell and the other savage. Then came another overthrow and another upward turn, during which he perceived still another Indian running toward them with uplifted gun. Then once more he was underneath, and his throat was seized in a grip of steel.

There came a crashing sound; the throttling grasp relaxed, and yet again Hubert twisted himself over and threw his enemy beneath him. But now what was his amazement to find his antagonist dead and limp in his hands. Springing to his feet and seizing his rifle, Hubert confronted the Indian he had seen approaching; and, to his utter bewilderment, recognized Blue Feather, his friend and comrade. Both of the Creeks lay dead on the ground—the one who had nearly slain Captain Blaisdell having a bullet through the breast from the young Shawnee's rifle, and Hubert's enemy a broken skull.

Captain Blaisdell was unhurt, it seemed, though he still lay on the ground, panting from utter exhaustion. Hubert was nearly helpless from the same cause, but he, too, was unable to show a wound of any sort to prove his near approach to death. For two or three breathless minutes the trees of the forest madly whirled about him, and he found it hard to believe that he was still alive and whole.

Meanwhile the main body of the Tennesseeans had advanced another furlong through the forest, driving the Indians before them. Presently the captain and Hubert were able to sit on a fallen log and to hear Blue Feather's account of the battle in other quarters of the field, and the way he had been able to come to their rescue.

Under cover of the artillery attack on the log fort, General Coffee had been able to occupy the river bank on the farther side without opposition. Just across the stream and within the horseshoe bend that formed the Indian stronghold they could see a hundred or more canoes, drawn up on the bank. These had evidently been prepared in readiness for the Creeks' retreat if they were driven from their fastness.

After waiting half an hour in idleness, some of the friendly Indian scouts proposed that they be allowed to swim the river and secure these canoes. General Coffee gladly gave his consent; the Indians took to the water, and soon had all the craft in their possession without having lost a man or raised any alarm. The scouts returned with the canoes; and Coffee quickly embarked a large portion of his command for an assault on the Indian position from the rear.

At the Creek village in the bend Coffee's men found only the women and children with a few old or partly disabled warriors. These were quickly overcome and made prisoners, and the huts were set on fire. This was the diversion which made possible General Jackson's victorious assault on the log wall. Since that time Coffee's force had been closing in on the savages from the rear, while the main body forced them backward through the wood. Caught thus between two lines of skillful and determined marksmen, the Creeks were utterly overwhelmed. Blue Feather declared that by this time not a hundred remained alive; and these were already surrounded in a dense undergrowth in the farthest extremity of the bend.

By the time Captain Blaisdell, with Hubert and Blue Feather, had rejoined the Rangers, the fate of this desperate remnant of the savage band had already been sealed. The scouts had set fire in three places to the thicket which sheltered them; and the Creek warriors were being driven forth by the flames, only to fall before the unerring rifles of the frontiersmen. Sometimes a group of two or three gained the river bank and plunged into the water. But they never reached the opposite side, for the men whom Coffee had stationed there before crossing to the village shot them down in midstream. The lives of the women and children were saved; but, at the end of that fierce battle in the Alabama forest, hardly more than a score of the hostile braves survived. The Redsticks, with nearly all their chiefs and the medicine men, who in howling tirades had promised them victory, had perished at the hands of the borderers.

# CHAPTER XIII

## THE HORSE THIEF

THE Dominion Rangers, with Hubert and Blue Feather, rode back to Tennessee in the wake of the victorious general. At Nashville many of the volunteers asked and received their discharges, but General Jackson prevailed on some of the best of his troops to remain with the colors through the summer and fall.

"Why, men!" he besought them in one of his impassioned harangues, "we've beaten the Creeks so that they'll never be the danger to our homes that they have been; but, even so, our work is only half done. There are the Spaniards in Florida, taking in the refugees and arming them, and at Pensacola sheltering the British force that set them on in the first place and found them arms and powder. We can never rest while that state of affairs continues. And any day we may expect to hear of a British fleet and army at the mouth of the Mississippi, ready to come up the valley and take the whole river away from us. If we don't block that move, what else will Tennessee and Kentucky be, five years from now, but British dependencies?"

Nearly the whole of Blaisdell's troop was among those who remained under arms. The captain projected a brief visit to his home in Virginia, and Hubert and

Blue Feather were to accompany him. But in June Old Hickory was appointed a major general of the United States Army and placed in command of the military district which included Tennessee and the Alabama territory. He was ordered to return to the Creek country and sign a treaty with the beaten tribe; and he designated the Rangers as a part of the force to accompany him. So the Virginia excursion was perforce abandoned.

Until this decision was actually reached, Hubert had not realized how he was counting on this visit to the plantation—on expressing to Mrs. Blaisdell his gratitude for all her kindness, and on looking again into Margaret's dark, honest eyes. What a brave little comrade she had been—always ready to help to the utmost of her ability and with never a whimper at danger or hardship! And how pleasant it would be to be riding with her again among the Blaisdell woods and pastures! Most reluctantly he gave up the idea of making the journey alone and rejoining the troop at Nashville on the general's return.

There were many exchanges of letters instead. The story of the campaign which culminated at the Horseshoe was fully told; and Captain Blaisdell did full justice to Hubert's share in the hand-to-hand struggle in the thicket. Mrs. Blaisdell wrote in breathless thankfulness for the outcome, and with the usual eager questioning as to how much longer the war would last. And Margaret Windom sent three pages of closely-written script that Hubert carried to a favorite spot in the woods to read.

DEAR HUBERT DELAROCHE [it ran]: It was a terrible time while you were in those awful woods hunting the Indian tribe; but now that you are safely back in Nashville I guess I have started growing again. My mark on the doorpost here didn't move a bit all winter; but now it's gone up half an inch in the last two weeks.

You know I didn't use to like to hear you and Captain Barnstable talk about politics and the war, because everything you said was against what I believed. But last Sunday Captain Barnstable and Mr. Blanchard and his wife were here to dinner; and I just wished you could hear the talk and join in it. Mrs. Blaisdell has made me see how things are. Her father was in the Revolution, as an aide to General Washington; and she knows all about these things. We've got to beat the British now or they'll make colonies of us again and make us pay the tea tax and everything like that. My mother's brother, Thomas Quincy, was killed fighting the British at Monmouth; and I'm going to be just as good an American as he was.

There was more—about the twin colts at the stables and the old saddle mare, Dolly, that had almost become Margaret's own—the girl pupils and their funny difficulties with French pronunciation, and last, and most important, the grand ball at Richmond in honor of Jackson's victory which Mrs. Blaisdell and all the girls had attended as spectators.

And, what do you think? They made us guests of honor on account of Captain Blaisdell being there. And I told every one I talked with about you, and the wonderful things you've done. Captain Blaisdell is splendid, I know, but he wasn't the only one that beat the Indians.

125

In August the treaty with the beaten Creeks was signed on the Hickory Ground. And Hubert, seeing the patient and manly bearing of the chiefs, many of whom had not taken part in the war, found it in his heart to be sorry that they were forced to accept such drastic terms. Two thirds of their lands were taken away, for the benefit of white settlers and to form a broad intervening area between their remaining towns and the Seminoles of Florida and the British agents who had established themselves in that territory. As in so many treaties following bitter fighting, the innocent and well-meaning ones of the beaten race were punished equally with the guilty.

On returning to Nashville Hubert renewed his request for a furlough during which the journey could be made to Virginia. But now the mind of the commander was full of other plans; he talked of nothing but the British schemes of conquest and the measures which must be taken to offset them. He was in daily conference with his trusted lieutenants, and a thousand details were found to demand the attention of Captain Blaisdell and the other company officers. A seven-day leave was the most that Hubert and Blue Feather could secure, and this being far too short for the ride to the plantation, they planned instead a deer-hunting trip to the Walden Ridge country, two days' journey to the eastward.

So it came about that on a late September afternoon Hubert was walking rapidly through a scattered wood of pine on a sunny hillside in that favored region and looking toward a recent clearing surrounding a little log house and barn in the valley below. He and his Indian comrade had established camp and picketed their horses in a grassy glen six or eight miles higher in the ridge. Game was abundant, and they had already hung the carcasses of two fine bucks from the branch of the great sugar tree that shaded their shack of boughs. But they had found their supply of meal running low, and before parting that morning to hunt on separate trails had agreed to procure some, if possible, at any settler's cabin which they chanced to find.

With his mind on the campaign he knew Old Hickory was planning, Hubert was scarcely conscious of his immediate surroundings. His gun was held carelessly at his side; his steps avoided, seemingly without volition, any obstacles in his way; and he felt rather than saw the perfection of the autumn landscape wherein the rich, dark green of the forest pines contrasted beauteously with the lighter emerald of the valley fields.

Without a moment's warning a rifle shot shattered the woodland silence. A bullet screamed viciously, and the hunter's hat was swept from his head and fell among the leaves ten feet away.

As quickly as though the missile had pierced his brain, Hubert fell at full length on the ground. Then, without the loss of a second, he wormed his body to the shelter of a low rock a short distance in front of him. It was not for nothing that he had fought the Creeks

in the Alabama forests. He had not the least idea why
he should be thus murderously assaulted in this peaceful
grove; and his pulses were pounding madly with the
realization of his peril; but his reaction was unhesita-
tingly that which it would have been in the midst of
the Redstick fastnesses. Peering cautiously over the
edge of the stone at a point where its contour was hidden
by low bushes, he scanned the ground ahead and for a
hundred paces on either side for some trace of his
assailant.

That the would-be assassin was alone he felt sure
from the fact that only one shot had been fired and
from the utter silence that followed it. His enemy
was hidden within a dozen rods of where he lay; and
if he found opportunity to reload his weapon would
surely repeat his attempt, perhaps with truer aim. For
two or three minutes Hubert's gaze searched the sunlit
slope before him, scrutinizing in turn each darker patch
or line that might betoken a human presence and noting
every swaying autumn branch and fluttering chickadee.
Meanwhile his rifle was ready at hand, with fresh powder in the pan and hammer at full cock.

At last, behind the trunk of a young pine, some
twelve or fourteen inches through, and about ten rods in
front of him, the hunted hunter saw a movement which
he instantly understood. A buckskin-clad upper arm
and elbow twice appeared and disappeared in an utterly
familiar motion. A man was standing behind that
tree, reloading his gun while using every precaution to

HUBERT'S GAZE SEARCHED THE SUNLIT SLOPE BEFORE HIM.

remain unseen. Already he was ramming down the powder charge. In ten seconds more the bullet also would be in place.

Like the glow from a lightning flash on a summer evening was Hubert's realization of the situation that confronted him. Leaping up from behind his shelter, he cleared the rock at a bound, and charged like a wounded stag straight at the tree trunk that sheltered his enemy. The would-be slayer heard his approach, and, before Hubert had covered half the intervening distance, sprang away from the tree and fled down the hillside with a yell of utter terror. He was a white man, it seemed—a tall thin figure, with long, graying hair and clad in soiled and ragged buckskins.

"Stop!" called Hubert, leveling his rifle at the fleeing figure. "Stop, or I'll shoot."

For answer the fugitive flung away his gun and did his best to redouble his speed. Hubert thundered on down the slope scarcely thirty paces behind. Since his own life was no longer in immediate danger, he would not shoot down his assailant as he easily might have done. Instead he was determined to take him alive and to solve the mystery of his unprovoked attack. Terror lent wings to the feet of the mountaineer, but Hubert was a runner who had found few equals among his comrades anywhere, and he was in perfect condition for a race for any stakes. Little by little the distance lessened between them. Panting and groaning, the fugitive dodged and doubled about to confuse his pursuer's aim, and sought by every means to keep some tree trunk or other obstacle between them. This effort proved his undoing at last, for turning momentarily to note Hubert's position, he caught his foot in a projecting root and plunged headlong to the ground.

A second later Hubert was upon him, pinning his body to the earth.

"Now tell me who you are," he shouted, "and why you tried to kill me."

The mountaineer lay gasping painfully and helplessly; and Hubert, perceiving that his fallen adversary was far slighter than himself and that he had no knife or other weapon, rose and hauled him to his feet as a constable might raise a drunken rowdy. Holding him firmly by the wrist, he repeated his demand.

"Why wouldn't I try to kill ye?" whined the prisoner at last. "Who c'n blame me if I did? Didn't you steal my hoss only this mawnin'—the only crittur I had to move a step on?"

"Steal your horse?" echoed Hubert in amazement. "I certainly did not. I never saw you or this place here before. What are you talking about?"

"Warn't you one o' them sojers along o' Bill Truden?"

"Bill Truden! I never heard of any such person. Are you drunk, man, or crazy?"

"No, I ain't drunk nor crazy nuther," declared the mountaineer, rubbing his eyes the while with the back of his free hand and gazing pitifully into his accuser's face, "but I donno' but I *be* mistaken. My eyes ain't noways so good as they used ter be, else I'd never missed ye clean, the way I did jest now. But the' was two sojers come this mawnin' inter my paster' over there—two sojers and Bill Truden, the old whisky maker an' claim jumper that seemed ter be kinder leader of 'em. He thought nobody'd know him over'n these parts. But *I* knew him—the old devil! I seen him once, years ago, when they was puttin' him in jail over in Kentucky; and I allus remembered him."

"Did they steal your horse?"

"Yes, they did, they sholy *did*. They come inter my paster' an' had jest caught my hoss 'n was puttin' a bridle on him when I come along on the jump. I'd seen 'em from where I was a workin' over in the corn lot. An' I says, 'Here you, that's my hoss. You let him be.' An' Bill Truden he jest kinder laughed—meanlike, the way he does—an' he says, 'Now look here,' he says, 'my pardner here,' pintin' to one of the sojers with him— 'he's got ter have a hoss. His hoss broke his leg in a chuck hole last night 'n we had ter shoot him. We'll jest borry your nag fer a while,' he says, ' 'n then we'll send him back—long 'bout winter strobry time,' he says. 'An' now,' he says, 'you jest shut yer face'n be peaceable,' he says, 'an' you won't git hurt.'

"What could I do? The' was three of 'em, an' they all had guns, an' I hadn't nothin' with me but an ax. So they jest took my hoss away in spite er me. I went right over ter the house ter git my gun, meanin' ter trail

133

'em up an' git one or two of 'em. But my old woman's down with the misery—ain't be'n able ter stir fer much as a week now. She begged an' prayed me not ter go; an' so at last I give it up."

"And when you saw me," questioned Hubert, "you thought I was one of that crew?"

"Yes, I sholy did. The' ain't be'n no other fellers in sojer's clo's 'round here fer I donno' when. An' when I see you I thought, 'Here's one of 'em comin' back ter see what else he c'n git. Wal, I'll *show* him what he'll git.' "

Hubert relaxed his grasp on his prisoner's wrist.

"I believe you're telling me the truth," he said heartily. "You've had terribly bad luck; and I wish I could help you. Your wife's sick, you say?"

"Yes," answered the mountaineer, miserably. She's be'n down on the flat of her back fer a week now, with the rheumatiz. An' I'd orter go ter Nashville or some place ter git some medicine fer her. Hold on!" he shouted. "There's another one—" And he pointed eagerly through the woods to where a tall man was striding toward them, rifle in hand, and with a pair of turkeys swinging at his sides, suspended by a cord from his neck.

Hubert grasped his rifle again, but immediately recognized the approaching hunter, and called to him loudly:

"Oh, Blue Feather, here's a man in trouble. Come and tell me whether we can help him."

Then in lower tones, to the mountaineer, "This is my partner, Blue Feather—a friendly, and one of General Jackson's scouts. He can help you if any one can."

By this time the young Indian had joined them, and Hubert quickly related the happenings of the last few minutes and the miserable plight of the mountaineer. "Now do you think we can do anything about getting that horse back?" he concluded.

"Where was he taken?" said Blue Feather. "And how long ago?"

"This mawnin'—'bout 'leven o'clock, mebbe, an' right out er my paster' over here," replied the settler eagerly.

"We'll go and look at the tracks they've left," said Blue Feather slowly. "We couldn't trail them far to-day, for it will soon be dark, and besides we have no horses here. But we'll see how they went, then go to our camp up there and come back in the morning. If they think no one is following, they may not travel far, and we may come up on them."

"That's mighty fine o' you," responded the mountaineer joyfully. "Mebbe you c'n kill two-three er them varmints 'n git my crittur back. Ef yer do, the' ain't nothin' I wouldn't do fer yer to pay yer back, though I ain't any money, as you c'n see plain enough. My name's Dave Lipton, 'n though mebbe I ain't no great shakes, I sholy can remember it when any one's done me a good turn."

"You won't need to pay us in any way," said Hubert

quickly. "We'll do what we can, though I don't want any one to be killed if I can help it."

"All right, stranger," answered Lipton, happily. "You do what yer can, an' I'll be satisfied. You're a *man*. I c'n see that *plain*. You sholy ain't one to lay up hard feelin's 'count o' my little mistake a spell ago. An' if you take after them varmints the way yer did after *me*, I guess they won't git clean away. Howsomever, if I's you, I wouldn't be *too* careful not ter hurt 'em. We got more er that sort'n we need anyhow."

"Well, we'll see," replied Hubert. "Now let's go and get your gun where you dropped it, and the hat that you lifted off my head; and then you can show us where they took the horse. We'll start after them early in the morning."

True to their word, the young hunters were back at the mountain pasture and on the trail of the thieves before sunrise. It was clear that Bill Truden had anticipated no pursuit, for the tracks were as plain as could be among the leaves of the wood and in the turf of grassy valleys, and there had been no effort to confuse possible followers by riding on flat ledges or along the beds of streams. So the trailers were able to go forward much of the time at a swinging trot, and before noon came upon the remains of the camp where the Truden gang had passed the night.

Pausing but half an hour to broil some venison and to rest and bait their mounts, they pushed on as before, through open woods and swales, along rocky hillsides and through the undergrowth of narrow ravines, until near nightfall, when they were riding on a darkening easterly slope, Blue Feather suddenly held up his hand and drew his mount to a halt. Hubert immediately halted also, and, without any questioning words, looked to his companion for an explanation of his gesture.

Presently the Indian youth backed his horse till he stood even with Hubert's, then asked in a low tone:

"Don't you smell it?"

"Smell what?"

"Their fire."

Thereupon Hubert took two long breaths of the light wind that was blowing in their faces, and plainly discerned the odor of wood smoke.

"Yes," he answered. "How far away is it?"

"Maybe half a mile," said Blue Feather. "I think it will be well to tie the horses in the thick woods there and to go forward a little way without them."

Ten minutes later the hunters found themselves approaching on hands and knees a narrow, rocky valley where, by the side of a clear stream, the horse thieves had pitched their camp. On the rims of the gulch there were but few trees, but great, rugged boulders and irregular patches of bush and thorn afforded nearly as secure a shelter and enabled the pursuers to approach in the gathering darkness within fifty yards of the camp fire without too great danger of detection.

Bill Truden, a heavy-shouldered and powerful man of sixty, with an unkempt, iron-gray beard, and wearing the buckskins of a frontiersman, was dressing some game near a rude stone fireplace; and two younger men in soldiers' uniforms were bringing wood and water from farther up the valley. Rifles and harness were lying about, and three horses were picketed near at hand. One of these, a gaunt, bay gelding, the lads quickly identified as Lipton's property by the white forehead star and the four white feet by which his owner had described him.

The three men were talking at intervals, but, as they spoke in low tones, but few of their words reached the ears of the watchers; and in the flickering lights and shadows their faces could not be plainly seen. It was evident that the soldiers had but little experience of backwoods ways, and more than once Truden jeered at them for some clumsy act or crude suggestion. Meanwhile he went on swiftly with the preparation of a meal, and soon was carving thick slices with his belt knife from the venison he had broiled over the coals.

Each of the men took up one of these on a sharpened twig, and all crouched about the fireplace, eating the meat with some pieces of hard biscuit which the soldiers took from their pouches. Apparently they had no coffee, but one of the men produced a whisky flask. This was passed around, and each in turn took a long drink. Then, at Truden's roughly voiced suggestion, the flask was stowed away in one of the saddlebags.

After ten minutes had passed Blue Feather attracted his companion's attention with a cautious touch on the

138

shoulder, and motioned with his head in the direction from which they had come. Hubert, instantly comprehending, noiselessly turned and crawled after him until they had placed a hundred yards or more between them and the camp and could rise to their feet. Thereupon the two made their way swiftly back to the thicket where their horses were hidden; and over some cold provision, taken from their saddlebags, proceeded to discuss the situation and to formulate their plans.

"There is no grass where their horses now stand," began Blue Feather, "and you will see that they will picket them for the night in that little meadow just up the stream from the fireplace. We will wait for three or four hours for the men to go to sleep. Then I will come down into the meadow from the woods over there, and lead or ride the stolen horse away. The valley walls are steep just there; and that is why this Truden has chosen the place—as one where their horses will not be likely to stray or to be stolen. But I marked one place where, with good luck, I can lead one up the bank; and once well out of sight, I'll risk their finding me."

"And what am I to do meanwhile?" demanded Hubert.

"You can stay by our horses here," replied Blue Feather, calmly. "And perhaps be ready to ride hard when I join you."

"Humph!" groaned Hubert, "that's a proper plan, I *must* say. You are to take all the risk, and I am to stay here by the horses. That's not the way I'd plan it."

"What would you do then? Surely one man can steal a horse as well as two—perhaps better, for he will make less noise."

"And what if they see you?"

"They will be sleeping."

"I'm not so sure of that. They may keep watch."

"I don't think so. They will be tired, and they do not believe any one is following them. If they did, they would ride differently."

"Well, I must go with you anyway," declared Hubert. "I won't hear to your going alone."

"Well," said the scout, reluctantly, "you might go with me a part of the way. It will be easy in the darkness. But I will leave you where I must crawl as the turtle does, for you cannot help me. It would be better, though, if you would stay here and wait for me."

Hubert shook his head; and his companion, finding him determined, ceased talking and turned to make such provision as was practicable for their own mounts. Since it was not safe to picket them to graze in the open, the lads pulled armfuls of grass from an intervale near by and so managed to feed them. Then the comrades seated themselves on a pile of leaves, with their backs against a great rock which had been warmed by the afternoon sun, and silently awaited the time for their attempt on the camp of the thieves.

The night was moonless, but the sky was clear overhead, and the stars afforded quite light enough for their venture. In this complete inaction the time dragged unbelievably. Indeed, so slowly passed the hours that it seemed to Hubert that it must be near midnight when at last Blue Feather rose, and, reaching for his rifle, set off without a word toward the bivouac in the ravine. Hubert followed close behind till they came in sight of the fire, whereupon the young Indian crouched among the grass and leaves and motioned to his companion not to accompany him farther.

For a quarter of an hour Hubert stood gazing in the direction in which the scout had disappeared. Then he heard a murmur of voices from the direction of the campfire and realized with a start that the night was not so far advanced as they had supposed, and that Truden and his companions were not yet asleep. Blue Feather's enterprise, if too soon attempted, might end in disaster. Probably he would hide among the trees on the other side of the ravine until the men in the camp were soundly sleeping. Yet he was counting on the remaining hours of darkness as their opportunity to put many miles between them and possible pursuit; and if he saw the horses wholly unguarded he might not delay. As Hubert realized this he ardently wished that he were again at his friend's side to warn him against rashness.

Except for the low murmur of voices at the fireplace, the night was utterly still; and as time passed Hubert grew more confident that Blue Feather would delay.

At last he decided to go back for a hundred paces or so under the trees where he might pass the intervening time in some measure of ease. Then once more the persistent fear for his comrade's safety assailed him, and at last became too sharp to be borne in complete inaction. For a minute or two he tramped back and forth in painful indecision; then he went down on his hands and knees in the grass and started to crawl toward the camp fire.

The voices grew clearer as he approached; some of the words became audible, and he made out something as to the distance to the Kentucky line. Then some quality in the voice of one of the speakers stopped him abruptly. He knew that voice—or he had known it. It was associated with some hateful episode, some ugly happening, the half-realized memory of which made him clench his hands and grind his teeth together as though in sudden rage. Where had he heard those tones before? That the speaker was his enemy he was sure, but his name he could not recall, no matter with what strained attention he listened. Forgetting all else, Hubert crawled swiftly toward the fireplace. He was now on the opposite side of the gulch from that where, in all probability, Blue Feather was hiding, and much nearer to the horse thieves. Gaining the shelter of a friendly boulder, he peered around it and saw the men still sitting or lying in slovenly attitudes and wholly unconscious of his approach. Thus reassured, he slipped forward to a place behind another and larger stone, a little to the left, and found himself within thirty paces of the group about the coals and able to hear clearly what they were saying.

Then again that maddeningly familiar voice:

"But what're you goin' to do with him, Truden, so's not to git into trouble?"

"Oh, don't worry 'bout that," replied the old claim jumper, "I'll fix that all right. Soon's we git over the line into Kentucky the' won't be no trouble 'bout where he come from. The' won't be no questions asked over there."

"And will you sell him then?" persisted the soldier.

Truden made some reply and in the same tones as before, but Hubert never knew what it was for the other man had moved a little nearer the fire so that the dying glow of the coals illumined his face, and Hubert's eyes and all his thoughts were fixed upon it. It was the face of John MacBean.

He was stooping now and drawing a blanket from beneath his saddle.

"Well, I'll turn in, I guess," he said with a yawn.

Truden leaned forward and poked at the fire with a stick. Dislodging a small live coal, he flung it upward, and caught it in the palm of his hand. Rolling it swiftly about on that leathery surface, he deftly transferred it to the bowl of his pipe, and, puffing vigorously, soon had the tobacco alight. Then he leaned back luxuriously and sent a slow succession of smoke wreaths into the air above his head.

143

MacBean spread his blanket on the ground near the fire, and, lying down, rolled himself snugly within it. The conversation and movement near the fire having ceased, the little valley was utterly still; and Hubert found opportunity to glance about the camp ground, to note the slumbering form of the other soldier and that the position of the horses in the tiny intervale was just what Blue Feather had predicted.

Then the behavior of one of the animals riveted the watcher's gaze upon him. The bay gelding was moving very slowly out of the range of the firelight, not with the closely restricted motion of an animal on a short picket rope—in a straight line rather, and exactly as though he planned an escape to be accomplished by such slow and imperceptible degrees as to avoid arousing the attention of his captors.

Hubert's first thought was that the animal had somehow loosened the stake to which he was picketed and was moving up the valley in search of fresher feed. But the motion was far too deliberate for that. It was as though the poor beast, having found himself at liberty, was clever enough to understand that rapid movement away from the camp would lead to his instant recapture. For a moment Hubert was filled with admiration for this almost human strategy. Then the truth burst upon him. The horse was not moving of his own volition. On the other side of his body, completely sheltered from the faint rays of the firelight, but guiding the animal's every movement, was Blue Feather,

144

the scout. No wonder the horse seemed likely to disappear as gradually and silently as a shadow when the sun goes down!

But now Bill Truden sat up and knocked the coals from his pipe. Yawning hugely, he threw another stick on the fire, then stood erect and rubbed the small of his back with the palm of his hand. The new fuel was dry, and blazed up at once, lighting the surrounding rocks and trees with a bright, unsteady glow. At that instant his gaze happened to rest on the horses and the slowly moving form of the gelding twenty paces beyond. Instantly he stiffened like a fighting dog at sight of his enemy and for five tense seconds stood peering through the murk, the whites of his eyes and his yellowed and broken teeth gleaming in the firelight. Then with a muttered oath he seized the rifle that leaned against a stone near by, threw back the hammer and leaped like a panther toward the intervale.

When Hubert read on Truden's face that the scout's effort to retrieve the stolen horse had been discovered he was fairly paralyzed with fear for his comrade's life. But when the freebooter, with plainly evident and deathly intent, sprang up the glen toward Blue Feather, resolve and action followed one another as the report of a flint-fired gun follows the click of its lock. Raising his rifle, Hubert fired instantly, and sent a bullet whistling two feet over Truden's head. Then he yelled at the top of his lungs—uttering the long-drawn, blood-curdling war-cry of the Creeks, and sending reverberating echoes up and down the valley till the outcry was like that which accompanies the onslaught of half a hundred painted savages.

The effect was magical. Truden stopped in his tracks, whirled about and flung himself behind a stone, and MacBean and the other soldier, who had sprung up and seized their weapons at the first alarm, made haste to follow his example. No hostile Indians were known to be in this region; but the massacre at Fort Mims and the bloody struggles of Jackson's campaign were too fresh in the minds of all the backwoods people to allow them to reason, while listening to the echoes of the war whoop, that there could be no war parties within a hundred miles of the ridge. Ten seconds followed during which the freebooters sought to avail themselves of any shelter from the expected volley, and Hubert from behind his stone saw a rider throw one leg and one arm over the bay gelding's back, drive him at a canter up the bush-lined path on the farther side of the ravine and disappear in the woods beyond.

Immediately Hubert began crawling backward as fast as he could go, being utterly careful meanwhile to keep the stone that had sheltered him between his body and the camp. His rifle was empty, but his pistol was ready; and he hoped to stop with this any rush of their enemies in his direction. Presently he was able to turn around and crawl more rapidly in the darkness toward the friendly shadow of a thicket of pines. This refuge gained, he stood erect and made his way swiftly and silently toward the place where he and Blue Feather had left their horses, recharging his piece as he went. He could discern no signs of pursuit, and five minutes later rejoined his comrade at their rendezvous.

Blue Feather had already unhitched the horses, and on Hubert's arrival wasted no breath in explanations. Springing to his saddle, with the halter rope of the recovered gelding in his hand, he rode away at a rapid pace in the direction from which they had come in the afternoon. Hubert followed close behind, with his rifle ready and his eyes turned toward the rear to note whether they were being followed.

In this fashion they rode for a quarter of an hour; then the scout urged his horse to a trot, and in the more open spaces they rapidly covered the ground. Blue Feather's course was chosen in no such careless fashion as that of Truden's party had been: advantage was taken of every opportunity to ride in the beds of streams; and twice they doubled on their tracks and retraced their way for half a mile or more. He never seemed to hesitate for the right direction, though once or twice he glanced at the stars as they crossed an intervale; and Hubert had no doubt that the most was being made of the advantage gained. So they traveled through the whole night, and paused to rest their mounts only when at dawn they found themselves within two hours' ride of the Lipton clearing.

Blue Feather declared that, even if Truden and his crew had quickly discovered that they were not the victims of an Indian raid, and determined to follow them, the thieves would have been wholly unable to trail them in the darkness and must therefore be nearly the whole distance behind. Nevertheless, he selected as a stopping place a thicket on a hilltop which commanded a view of a mile or more of the way on which they had come; and, even as he ate or talked, maintained a constant lookout. As he had predicted, no pursuers appeared; and by nine o'clock the two youths rode into the Lipton farmyard with the recovered animal trotting contentedly beside them.

## CHAPTER XIV

### ABINGTON

IN October General Jackson set out from Nashville with a strong body of militia and regulars, and wholly on his own responsibility, to attack the town of Pensacola in west Florida where the Spaniards had permitted a British force to occupy the fort and dominate the nearby territory. On the seventh of November the town was taken and the fort destroyed, the British garrison having been driven aboard the warships in the bay.

Ten days later Old Hickory was at Mobile, in the Alabama territory, accompanied by two regiments of regular troops and a small body of scouts and riflemen, among whom were numbered Captain Blaisdell's troop of Rangers. Less than ever did Hubert feel that the work of the southwestern army was completed. Rumors every day became more persistent and detailed that a powerful British force was being made ready for the attack on New Orleans; soldiers, sailors and backwoodsmen everywhere repeated them; and not a day passed that the General did not send urgent messages to Knoxville or to Washington. With the contents of some of these Hubert was acquainted, through the discussions openly held among the officers; and it gradually became clear that the fierce war with the Creeks, of which he had seen the culmination, and the taking of Pensacola were only preliminary skirmishes in a campaign that might prove the greatest of the war.

Volunteers began to appear at the Mobile encampment in groups of two or three or more, from the backwoods forests and farms and the ships in the bay. Presently this motley crew of sailors, hunters and adventurers was organized into a company of infantry, and set to drilling under a captain and other officers from the regular regiments. Of these operations Hubert was a keenly interested spectator; and every day he spent as many hours on the edge of the drill ground as he could possibly get free from other occupations. Thus far he had had but little experience of regular military training; and he meant to learn as much as possible in anticipation of the time of his enrollment.

On the third day, when he had been thus employed for an hour or two, he became conscious of the fact that for five minutes he had been watching the movements of one of the recruits to the exclusion of those of all the others.

This was a tall and somewhat thin and lank individual of fifty or more, with a clean-shaven, deeply wrinkled countenance and hair so closely cropped as to make its color almost indistinguishable. The neatness of his person and dress distinguished him in some

150

measure from the rough sailors and backwoodsmen with whom he was associated, but the onlooker presently realized that the thing which had attracted his attention to this tall stranger was the latter's comparative skill and promptness in carrying out the orders given. The other men of the company, like all raw recruits, were slow and clumsy in executing the unaccustomed movements; but this man went through the manual and all the marching evolutions with the accuracy of a well-planned machine. It was perfectly evident that military drill was to him no new experience.

When Hubert had arrived at this natural explanation of the stranger's behavior it seemed that his curiosity should be satisfied, and he turned away to watch the evolutions of an awkward squad that was marching back and forth across the field under the direction of a hoarse-voiced and perspiring sergeant. Farther to the right a company of regulars was maneuvering; and, compared with their vigorous and well-timed movements, the efforts of the new recruits, with their straggling ranks, broken step and wavering, uncertain weapons, were well-nigh ridiculous. But in spite of all these elements of interest in the general scene, Hubert soon found that his gaze was again following the lanky recruit in the ranks of the Mobile volunteers. Surely there was something about him that compelled attention.

With some irritation at the persistence of this worrying suggestion, Hubert tried concentrating his looks and his thoughts on the man, in an effort to remember whether he had ever seen him before. Once, when the marching evolutions brought him to a stand within five or six paces, the lad fixedly stared at him for ten seconds or more and ran over in his mind the various places where he might have observed him; but all to no purpose—the resemblance to some one he had known, or whatever other circumstance it was that so enchained Hubert's attention, was illusory or vanishing. At times Hubert told himself that the recruit must be a brother or other close relative of some one he had known well in the past; at other times he was satisfied that this was mere self-deception, and that the man was notable only because of his accurate drilling. It was quite certain that the stranger saw nothing familiar in Hubert, for once when they met on a pathway in the camp ground his look was of utter blankness, and he passed without a word.

Next day Hubert was employed during the time the recent volunteers were at drill, but later paid a visit to their quarters where he was determined to make the acquaintance of this puzzling individual. A brief description of the one he sought, given to some other members of the company whom he met on the way, brought the information that the man's name was Abington, that they had first met him in Mobile just before General Jackson's arrival, and that he had been made a sergeant that very morning. Hurrying to the quarters of the lieutenant who had charge of the new company when it was not on the drill ground, Hubert learned, to his intense disappointment, that Abington had left Mobile only three hours before, in charge of a squad of mounted men that was being sent with messages to New Orleans. Evidently the man's ability was receiving recognition from his superiors; but the lieutenant either did not know or would not tell anything of who he was or whence he came. Beyond the words, "John Abington, Aged 50," the muster roll was equally useless as a source of information.

Hubert returned to his quarters, to find Captain Blaisdell impatiently awaiting his coming. New reports had arrived of the sailing of a great British fleet from the West Indies and through the Straits of Florida. The camp was already humming with excitement, and preparations of every kind were going forward for an early march to the Mississippi.

Within the next two weeks Old Hickory had effected this momentous change of base, and was encamped at New Orleans with all the troops he could collect. This was the strategic point for the control of the outlet and all the lower portion of the great waterway, and he had often declared that so long as American forces held it no hostile fleet or army could dominate the southwestern territory.

One morning, late in December, Hubert was walking across the camp ground at New Orleans and closely observing the scattered groups of recent recruits. He

153

had not seen Abington since he left Mobile; but his curiosity was still unsatisfied, and he meant to question the tall volunteer at the first opportunity, in the hope of learning the source of the tantalizing resemblance. That he was somewhere in the encampment Hubert knew from the reports of different members of the Mobile company; but the man was no longer with their organization, and was said to have been detailed for some special duty. Meanwhile no one seemed to know exactly where he could be found.

Thrilling events had rapidly followed one another since the arrival of Jackson's army. The persistent rumors of British invasion had been changed to certainty by the appearance in the narrow waters between Lake Borgne and the Gulf of Mexico of a fleet of fifty ships of war and a great number of transports, bearing, it was calculated, at least twelve thousand men with all their artillery and stores. A few days later the five little gunboats, which were the sole American force on the lake, were captured or destroyed, and the British commander proceeded to land a strong detachment of infantry with many heavy guns at the mouth of Bayou Bienvenu, less than twenty miles from New Orleans. This force had been rapidly increased, and, although delayed by difficulties of transport and by its officers' lack of knowledge of the country, had in the course of the next ten days pushed forward through the swamps to the Villeré Plantation, within three or four miles of the Mississippi at a point only ten miles below the city. Their movements had been seriously hampered by Jackson's policy of commandeering all draft animals, felling trees across all possible land and water routes and by the low stage of the water in the bayous. But, except for the gallant and hopeless struggle of the gunboats on the lake, they had met no armed resistance.

Meanwhile Old Hickory was assembling an army to oppose them, declaring martial law, sending red-hot messages to Natchez and Nashville for the delayed detachments of Tennessee and Kentucky militia, impressing reluctant Creoles, arming and drilling new levies and ransacking the city and the country roundabout for cannon of any sort to reënforce his scanty supply. By this, the twenty-third day of December, he had brought together a motley array of some twenty-two hundred men, of whom nearly two thirds were militia and volunteers. Many of the newer recruits were without uniforms or other insignia, and their weapons would have made up a perfect museum display of firearms, old and new and of every type and condition.

Hubert had learned that a desperately necessary feature of Jackson's strategy was the concealment from the British commander of the incredible weakness and unpreparedness of the American forces. Elaborate measures had been taken to impress the enemy leaders with the contrary belief, every pretense was maintained of the existence of a great and active force, and deserters and possible spies were sternly dealt with. On two occasions the stillness of early morning on the camp's outskirts had been shattered by the volleys of firing squads, and wretched individuals who had sought to earn British gold by espionage paid the penalty of their treason. General Pakenham's slow progress through the swamps and bayous to the south had been still further retarded by the supposed necessity for defending each advanced position against attack by a powerful army. Reconnaissance in force had not been thought practicable; and consequently the British General was even yet unaware of the most favorable routes for attack. In this situation every day and hour of delay was of advantage to the American cause. Additional forces and supplies were slowly coming in, and the raw troops were being beaten by ceaseless drilling into the semblance of an army.

It was the thought of possible spies and the terrible injury they might inflict which had reminded Hubert of the tall stranger he had observed at Mobile. Now he recalled, or thought he did, that on the one occasion when he had met this individual face to face there had been something sidelong and furtive in the way he had failed to meet his gaze. And the fact that no one could be found who knew anything of Abington's previous employment began to assume a sinister meaning. The more Hubert thought of the matter the more determined he became to solve the mystery of this man's presence in the army.

Suddenly, from behind the young messenger, and fifty yards to the left, came a jeering call:

"Yah! Blue Lighter! What'd you do with that girl you run away with?"

Wheeling about, Hubert saw two soldiers standing near one of the huts of a volunteer company and looking in his direction. Ten seconds' scrutiny of their faces revealed that the one who stood two paces in advance was Rowdy MacBean of New London, and that the other was the mulatto cook, Jim Brentford, who had deserted the *Bluebird* in the longboat of the Baltimore privateer.

Hubert stood in his tracks while the other advanced menacingly.

"What're you doin' here?" demanded MacBean. 'Goin' ter burn some more blue lights?"

"I never burned any blue lights," retorted Hubert. "And neither did my friends whom your crowd tried to murder. As for the girl, she's safe and in good company."

"Yah! you sneakin' Tory, you!" yelled MacBean, who had now approached within five paces. "Let you tell it, you're an angel!"

"That kind of talk comes well from a *horse thief*."

"Horse thief? What in the devil do you mean? Horse thief, am I? I've a good mind to break your face in right now."

For answer Hubert stripped off his hat and coat, flung them on the ground and turned to face his adversary. But MacBean did not at once advance to the attack. In the year that had elapsed since the fight on the New London street Hubert had grown an inch taller and thirty pounds heavier. The outdoor life and ample exercise of his employment had hardened his muscles, quickened all his movements and suffused his face and neck with a robust coat of tan. At the sight of Hubert's broad shoulders and sinewy arms and, above all, his air of perfect readiness, Rowdy visibly hesitated   Seeing this, Mulatto Jim, not to be balked of his hope of witnessing a battle, came forward to his side and shouted, gleefully:

"Give it to him.  Give it to him, Mist' MacBean. He d'serves it, every bit.  I heard him tellin' the cap'n on *me,* when I was leaving' the *Bluebird* boat.  An' if you can't give him what he ought to have, why then I will."

The mulatto was over six feet tall and strongly built.  Hubert remembered a scrimmage in the forecastle of the *Bluebird* in which the cook had proved more than a match for two of the other sailors.  The young messenger had fairly concluded that he was doomed to undergo a repetition of the affair in the New London street, from which he had barely escaped with his life, when he heard the sound of swiftly running feet and Blue Feather, rifle in hand, thrust himself between him and the mulatto.

"What's that you'll do?" demanded the Shawnee.

158

"If you move to lay a hand on *him* I'll let daylight through you."

Before the leveled gun and the scout's menacing, coal-black eyes, Mulatto Jim fell back hastily. But half a dozen more of the members of the company, attracted by the noise of the quarrel, came running to the scene.

"Come! Fair play here!" shouted a burly sergeant. "Man to man and no interference. Put down that gun, you redskin, or we'll take it away from you."

"Hi yi!" yelled another. "Form a ring here and see fair play. No weapons and no gouging. Come on, fellers."

In a twinkling Hubert and MacBean were facing each other in the center of a ring formed by the soldiers who now came running from all directions. Hubert crouched in readiness for Rowdy's attack, though he advanced not a step, for even now he determined not to be the first to strike. While the later comers pushed and elbowed for a better view of the coming fray Rowdy began again to curse and threaten, as if to overwhelm his enemy with imprecations. But his comrades quickly checked these loud-mouthed insults with yells of derision.

"Go at him, MacBean. Don't try to scare him to death. You can see he ain't that kind. Go *at* him."

Then, in the midst of the yells and jeers, and before a blow had been struck, there burst out a terrific clamor of bells and gongs from every part of the city. A hubbub arose in distant parts of the camp and a roar of drums. An officer was seen riding at breakneck speed from the direction of headquarters.

"Hold on! hold on, boys," cried the sergeant, "let's see what this is."

The soldiers turned to face the messenger who was now almost upon them. Waving his hat, he shouted:

"Fall in line, men. Where are your officers? The British are coming. They're on the river bank, and they'll be here in no time if we don't check them. Oh, there's the captain!"

"Captain," he went on to a disheveled and hatless man who came running from the cabins, sword in hand, "form your company at once, and report at the *Place des Armes*. The enemy is coming forward."

"Right!" bellowed the captain. "Get your guns and fall in line, men. Where are the drummers? Let them sound the assembly."

Instantly the group broke up, the volunteers, including MacBean and Brentford, running toward their quarters for their weapons. The General's aide galloped off to carry his message to a group of officers who awaited him at a little distance. Hubert and Blue Feather rushed away in other directions to spread the alarm and later to rejoin their company, weapons in hand. The bells continued to ring like mad, and the whole camp ground reëchoed with the hoarse shouts of officers and the furious beating of drums.

# CHAPTER XV

## WHEN GREEK MEETS GREEK

BY midafternoon nearly the whole American force was drawn up on the narrow plain of Chalmette, some six or eight miles south of the city. This half-mile strip of firm ground that intervened between the river on the west and an impassable cypress swamp on the east was the only practicable approach to New Orleans by the route the British commander had selected. To the rear of the American forces was the Canal Rodriguez, which stretched from the swamp to the river and which had already been seized upon by the defenders as the nucleus of an earthwork that might be pricelessly useful if a retreat became necessary. In this position the patriot army could not be outflanked, as both right and left wings rested on impassable barriers. Hubert was already soldier enough to understand and admire the strategy of his commander in selecting a position which gave to the weaker party, so long as it remained on the defensive, such solid advantages.

Less than half a mile down the plain, and in full view in the afternoon sunshine, the British regiments had come to a halt, and the soldiers under Old Hickory had abundant opportunity to note the colors of their uniforms—green for the rifles and red for the infantry of the line—the glittering lines of their bayonets and the perfect order and rhythm of all their movements. Officers in scarlet coats and glowing epaulets rode back and forth along the lines and mounted messengers trotted to and from the low buildings at the rear above which a general's flag had already been hoisted.

Major Harkness, who with his companies of Tennessee Volunteers and Virginia Rangers had been posted on the extreme right, had sent Hubert with a message to General Jackson, and the lad had halted his horse just outside a group of officers who were in close conference with the commander. Just then a line of skirmishers issued from the main body of the Redcoats and advanced rapidly toward the American position. Instantly every officer and man was on the alert; swords were drawn and rifle primings looked to. Everywhere could be heard the voices of the regimental and company commanders urging their men to hold their fire till the enemy was well within range. For the moment Hubert forgot his immediate errand and paused to see that his own weapon was in readiness.

But the skirmishers had advanced barely two hundred paces when their line was halted and by a succession of brisk orders transformed to a series of outposts, aligned as at a permanent camp ground. Then it was noted that the perfect formation of the regiments behind them had given place to a great number of moving groups. Muskets were stacked, and numerous individuals scattered toward the levee on the one hand or the swamp on the other and returned bearing armfuls of driftwood and branches.

"They're not going to attack," said the General. "Pass the word for the men to stand at ease."

At this Hubert pressed forward to the General's side and delivered the message from Major Harkness. General Jackson acknowledged this with a nod, but turned to some of his officers without replying.

"I believe they're building camp fires," said Major Latour, Chief of the Engineers. "Yes, look there. See that smoke. They're going to camp there for the night and attack us in the morning."

"No," said General Jackson, deliberately. "They're going to fight right there where they are, and to-night."

No one made any reply to this declaration, and the General turned to Hubert to say:

"Go tell the major that. Tell him to hold his position for the present; and I'll send him further orders."

Then to the staff officers around him:

"Go and tell Coffee and Carroll and the others the same thing. Then come back here at once. I want two of you to ride back to the city with me."

The little group dissolved, and Hubert returned to Major Harkness with the message he had been bidden to deliver. After a few minutes they saw the commander with two of his aides leaving the field along the cart road that followed the line of the levee.

Two hours later the three riders returned, the Gen-

eral's tall figure unmistakable even in the gathering
darkness. Aides were dispatched to right and left, and
there ensued a period of waiting even more tense than
that of the afternoon when the British assault had been
momentarily expected. A cold wind had sprung up and
a heavy fog drifted in from the river. Sometimes the
successive waves of this enveloping cloud were so dense
that it was impossible to distinguish human figures at
more than a dozen paces. Next moment the air would
be swept clear by the freshening breeze and the British
camp fires would again be plainly visible. The whole
scene was enwrapped in a mysterious silence—such an
absence of the sounds of voices, footsteps and all the
varied noises that naturally arise among throngs of
people of whatever intent that Hubert could hardly
realize his surroundings. The murmur of the night
wind and the sound of the ripples from beyond the
levee seemed more in keeping with an encampment of
a little group of travelers on the prairie or in the
wilderness than with the actuality of their situation.
For minutes together he gazed through the murk at
Captain Blaisdell and Lieutenant Green, who alone of
all his comrades were visible, and pleased himself with
this quaint imagining of a vast solitude surrounding
them.

Suddenly a horrible roar of guns shattered the silence
into a thousand quivering fragments. The terrific
sounds came from the direction of the river; and for a
moment Hubert thought that the British warships had

somehow managed to ascend the hundred miles of winding channel from the gulf and were now attacking the American army on the flank. Then came another clearing wind, and he made out, over the levee and a half a mile down the stream, the outlines of the American armed schooner, Carolina, which now lay broadside on, within four hundred yards of the British encampment. As he gazed in astonishment at this spectacle there came a sheet of flame from the vessel's rail and the roar of another broadside. This time it was evident that the schooner was sending her discharges almost point blank into the enemy position. Shrill cries arose in the British encampment and the loud and hoarse voices of officers.

Then from the darkness a little way to the left the sound of a well-known voice:

"Steady, men. Hold your positions. Be ready for the word."

"Steady, men. Steady," echoed the voices of officers all around them while the General and three of his aides rode by, not ten feet away. Three or four breathless minutes passed; then came another shattering discharge from the warship. Then another period of waiting while the sailors recharged their pieces, followed by another broadside. Three times more this was repeated; then three rockets, red, white and blue, went up from the vessel in quick succession. The instant the trailing sparks from the third had fallen into the inky waters of the river the voice of the General was heard again from the shadow of the levee and fifty yards in advance of the Rangers, where he headed a body of marines:

"Attention! . . . Forward . . . *march!*"

Quickly the word went up the line, to be instantly followed by the tramp of feet and the clank of weapons and accouterments. Ten minutes later the General, at the head of some twelve hundred men, had placed himself on the British left flank, between the levee and the red-coated regiments. The latter, though severely shaken by the cannonade, were drawn up in regular formation among their camp fires and were thus clearly visible to their enemies. No sentinels had been encountered by Jackson's men. Apparently the flank movements of the Americans were wholly unsuspected, for the British ranks faced toward the north rather than the west and no challenging fire was directed toward the levee. During the march from the position near the canal Hubert had learned that General Coffee, with most of the Tennessee and Mississippi volunteers, was executing a similar maneuver on the British right. Old Hickory's plan was to take the enemy's advanced force between two fires and complete the work so well begun by the broadsides of the Carolina.

In the deep shadow of the levee Jackson marched on until nearly the whole of his column was between the British encampment and the river. Then he faced his men to the left and instantly gave the order to charge.

## WHEN GREEK MEETS GREEK

Across the soft ground, in the dense murk of fog and shadow, the whole force went with a rush, firing as they ran with deadly effect at the scarlet figures so plainly outlined before them. The Redcoats faced about and fired at command into the darkness whence came these savage volleys, but very few of their bullets found living marks; and in a moment the attackers were upon them. There ensued a bitter struggle in which the torn and shaken British ranks were decimated by the bayonets of Jackson's regulars and the whirling rifle butts of the frontiersmen. In the midst of this fierce mêlée a crash of musketry on the other flank told that Coffee was carrying out his portion of the work. Nearly the whole American army was assaulting the British vanguard; and the cross fire to which the invaders were now subjected might well lead them to believe that they were being surrounded by an overwhelming force.

Hubert was riding by the side of Captain Blaisdell, and had emptied first his rifle, then his pistol, into the midst of the swaying groups of red-coated figures. Amid a pandemonium of yells and blows and a rain of bullets that seemed to come from every direction, the British formation was everywhere breaking down; and the Americans, seeing victory within their grasp, pressed forward all along the line.

But the men whom they were attacking were seasoned veterans of Wellington's campaigns. They had been amazed and shaken by the cannon fire; and the well-

167

aimed rifles of the charging infantry had taken a heavy toll; but they were not to be driven from the field like raw recruits, however surprising the attack that was launched against them. These were no half-hearted conscripts, herded to a war of which they knew not the cause and cared not for the end, but men who saw in the greatness and power of Britain the only surety against anarchy and despotism, and who had proved their mettle on a hundred hard-fought fields.

Here and there among the camp fires, in groups of two or three to a score or half a company, sometimes led by hatless and bleeding officers who were fighting, sword in hand, they stubbornly held their ground, and with flashing bayonets or no less deadly musket butts gave their assailants blow for blow.

Captain Blaisdell, with two or three of his troopers on his right and young Hubert Delaroche on his left, charged headlong into one of these desperate groups, · and a furious combat ensued. The captain swung a heavy sword, and Hubert whirled his little rifle about his head and warded desperate thrusts and blows. Men went down before him and around him, and others appeared from the murk like eerie figures of a frightful dream and fought on and on as gnomes or devils having lives immune to the strokes of any mortal weapons. Horses and men struggled and tramped through the blazing camp fires and scattered the embers over the muddy ground. The firelight rapidly lessened, and the enveloping mist rolled all about them, making the battlefield as dark as a midnight forest where no one could distinguish friend from foe.

Suddenly Hubert found himself confronted by a huge, dark figure with wildly swinging arms and sensed rather than saw the imminent stroke of a heavy weapon. By instinct, he thrust his left arm upward to protect his head and crouched in his saddle to lessen the blow's impact. There was a crash as of a cannon exploding close at hand, and a thousand vivid streaks of light flashed in every direction before his eyes as though the sky had been split asunder by an incredible thunderbolt. Then utter blackness and the sense of falling.

# CHAPTER XVI

## THE HAND OF COMRADESHIP

WHEN Hubert came to himself he was lying on a pile of loose cotton in the field behind the Canal Rodriguez. Near by stood Captain Blaisdell and Blue Feather who were talking in low tones. The rising sun was sending beams of red-gold light through the upper branches of the cypress trees of the swamp, and the figures of men and animals cast hugely lengthened shadows on the frost-rimed ground. On similar piles of cotton or of leaves and straw lay other prostrate figures, some in the homespun of the frontier or the regimentals of the regulars, and others in the scarlet or the blue of the invading army. Over these bent surgeons and their assistants with their instruments and bandages, and here and there a covered form on a litter was being borne away by silent and grim-faced soldiers.

The pervading sense of pain and bewilderment which was the first thing of which the young messenger was aware soon resolved itself into a fiercely throbbing ache at his temples and a slow oozing of blood across his cheek. For a minute or so he lay inert, gazing stupidly at his surroundings through half-opened eyes;

then a sudden remembrance of the events of the pre-
eeding night brought full consciousness and a devour-
ing eagerness to know the struggle's outcome.

"Did we beat the British?" he asked.

The sound of the words was surprisingly weak, for
Hubert's usually lusty voice seemed to have oozed
away with the blood from his hurts; but both Captain
Blaisdell and Blue Feather turned toward him at once,
and both knelt down at his side.

"He's coming to, thank God!" exclaimed the captain.

"Good! Good!" said the young Indian more fer-
vently than Hubert had ever heard him speak. "He
will be well again. The bone is not broken."

"We'll get the surgeon," returned the other. "He'll
have to sew up that wound."

"Yes," answered Blue Feather, "I go for him now."

Swiftly rising, he darted away in pursuit of a be-
spectacled individual who had been kneeling by the
side of a wounded British officer fifty paces away and
was now headed for the other side of the encampment. Captain Blaisdell dipped his handkerchief in a
pail of clear water that stood near by and began bathing the blood from Hubert's face.

"I knew you'd come 'round, boy," he said warmly.

"Yes," said Hubert, "but did we beat the British?"

"Yes, yes, we beat 'em off the field—drove 'em back
a mile and a half and held the ground for five hours.
Then their reënforcements were coming up, and I guess

the General didn't want 'em to see how few of us there were, so he brought us back over the ditch here; and we're throwing up earthworks. But don't worry about all that. When the surgeon has sewed up your wound we'll get you back to the town. You've done enough for this campaign."

"Oh, no, I haven't, captain. I want to see it through," answered Hubert, stubbornly. And in spite of the captain's frown and shaking head, he was still protesting this decision when Blue Feather returned with the surgeon who bade the wounded youth be still while he examined him.

After a few moments' scrutiny of the wide gash on the messenger's head and a grim but skillful probing of its vicinity with his finger ends, the man of medicine stood erect and said in a matter-of-fact tone to Captain Blaisdell:

"Bad scalp wound, that's all. Take five or six stitches."

Opening his field pack, he drew from it the materials for this simple operation, and with Captain Blaisdell's assistance in holding the edges of the fissure together, had soon completed the work. Then, catching sight of a great, blue swelling on Hubert's left forearm, he proceeded in a most business-like manner, and in utter disregard of the patient's grunts and winces, to probe and test this bruise for a possible fracture. Evidently he found none, for he presently rose from his knees again and said:

"Partly stopped that gun butt with your arm, didn't you? I was wondering how you escaped a broken skull. Well, they'll get you back to town on one of the wagons; and you just lie still for three days and be careful for a week or so more, and you'll be all right. You're a lucky boy, too. Now," he went on as he bent over to close his instrument case, "I've got to get along to some of these men that are worse off. Good morning, captain."

Hubert's friends soon found him a place on a mule-drawn wagon, the low body of which was half filled with cotton which served as a bed for several wounded men. The captain returned to his troop, which, with nearly the whole of the attacking force of the preceding night, now stood or lay behind the half-completed barrier in momentary expectation of an assault. A force of negroes was shoveling with might and main to raise the embankment, and a procession of wagons was bringing cotton bales to fill more quickly the lowest places in the line.

Blue Feather stalked by the side of the rude ambulance, frequently assuring himself that Hubert had not again lost consciousness and twice procuring fresh water for him and his wounded companions. In this way they came into the town and soon were reëstablished in their former quarters in a warehouse near the levee.

Four days later Hubert was walking abroad, though not permitted to return to duty. On New Year's Day a terrific sound of cannonading reached the city from the Plain of Chalmette; and he went half wild with the fear that the great battle for the possession of New Orleans was being fought without him. But after some hours the roar of artillery died away, and he learned from messengers riding from the field that the infantry had not been engaged, for the British regiments had not approached within rifle shot of the redoubt. The messenger gayly declared that the Redcoats had had much the worse of the artillery duel, having lost many cannoneers and heavy guns, while the Americans had escaped with little damage. Cotton bales, however, had proved a poor defense, as in several places they had been set on fire by red-hot cannon shot. As a consequence, the General had ordered the bales pulled out of the redoubt and replaced by more dependable earthwork and logs.

Next day, as Hubert was strolling along the levee, not far from his quarters, whom should he see approaching on the narrow pathway but Rowdy MacBean! Hubert's head was still swathed in a bandage; and now Rowdy was carrying his left arm in a sling. It was evident that he too had come to close quarters with the enemy in the night battle, and now bore an honorable wound.

Evidently there was some good in the man in spite of his ruffian talk and ways. As for the horse stealing, that, after all, had been the act of the old claim jumper, Truden; and perhaps, MacBean had really

174

thought at the time that the animal was to be returned to its owner.

With these thoughts in mind, and obeying a sudden impulse of comradeship, Hubert advanced with a smile on his face and with his right hand extended, and said:

"How are you, MacBean? I see you're wounded, too. Come now, let's shake hands and let bygones be bygones."

For an instant Rowdy hesitated and looked about him. Jim Brentford was sitting, pipe in mouth, at the window of a neighboring building, his elbows on the sill and his chin in his hands. MacBean ground his heel into the soft earth, spat contemptuously to one side, then with a sneer on his face turned away from the proffered hand.

"I guess you *would* be glad to let bygones be bygones," he growled, "but I ain't shakin' hands with a Blue Lighter—not if I know it. And I ain't forgot what you called me the other day, either."

Hubert's face grew very red, and for a moment he did not reply. Meanwhile MacBean sidled past as though his enemy were an ugly dog that might attack him without warning if he turned his back.

"Very well," said Hubert at last, in a tone that was husky with anger. "I can't make a proper answer to that as long as your arm is in a sling; but when it's mended, let me know, and I'll try to do so."

"Have it your own way," sneered Rowdy. "I know

who 'twas that shot Bill Barton at the Windom place
and sent him to the hospital for three months. If you
wasn't a pet of the officers here, I'd had you run out
of camp or stood up and shot long before this."

"All right," said Hubert, hotly. "You go tell that
story to the General or to any one else, and I'll face
the consequences. There are two sides to that affair.
I can tell mine, and I'm not ashamed of it."

"Oh, you go to—" growled the other, turning his
back contemptuously. "You think you're safe because
you've toadied up to some of the officers and made
'em think you're a little white lamb. But I'll git you
before I git through, and don't you fergit it."

Hubert stood in his tracks and watched MacBean
saunter down the levee and disappear in a little grog
shop near a landing a furlong away. For the first
time since he joined the army the young messenger
seriously considered the possibility of further trouble
for himself arising from the Blue Light episode at New
London. As he turned about and resumed his interrupted walk he encountered the leering smile of Mulatto Jim who still leaned on the window sill of the
old warehouse, puffing slowly at his pipe, in evident
enjoyment of the scene he had witnessed.

## CHAPTER XVII

### THE MOBILE VOLUNTEER

FIVE days after the meeting with MacBean
Hubert was again strolling about the town and
among the quarters of the newly arrived soldiers. The delays which General Pakenham's advance
had suffered from his lack of knowledge of the forces
opposing him and the surprising fierceness of the night
attack on his vanguard were proving of wonderful
advantage to the defenders of the city. While the
British struggled through the half-empty bayous between Lake Borgne and the river bank with boatloads
of heavy guns and solid shot and the paraphernalia
of siege warfare, the Americans were steadily raising
the embankment at Chalmette, fortifying a new position on the west bank to check a flanking movement in
that direction, and, best of all, receiving reënforcements of some thousands of riflemen from Kentucky
and Tennessee. With these additions Jackson's army
had come to total nearly six thousand men, and was
thus perhaps two thirds as numerous as that which
directly threatened him.

For a fortnight, in the midst of stirring events,
Hubert had not been concious of any thought of the
tall volunteer who had roused his suspicions at Mobile,
but that the stranger had not been wholly absent from

177

his mind was proved by the sudden jolt of surprise and apprehension which now followed the sight of him on the boundary of the camp ground. The man was hurrying along with his eyes bent on the ground. As usual, he seemed to pay but little attention to any whom he met, and neither to expect nor to desire any comradely greetings.

Instantly Hubert determined to follow this mysterious individual and to learn at least the location of his quarters and the names of his immediate superiors. For ten minutes or more the messenger hurried after him on this quest, leaving the camp ground behind and threading some of the crooked streets of the levee district of the town. Abington was striding along at a great pace, his long, vigorous limbs well serving in place of a mount; and Hubert, who was still somewhat languid with the effects of his wound, found it no easy task to keep him in sight. But just as he realized this and began to fear losing all track of the man, he was fortunate enough to catch sight of Blue Feather who had just landed from a small boat at one of the docks. A low whistle, in imitation of the call of a quail, that they had often used in signaling each other in the woods served to draw the young Indian's attention, and he came hurrying to Hubert's side, rifle in hand.

"See that man ahead there," said Hubert breathlessly. "I want to keep him in sight. I'm afraid he's a spy."

"Leave him to me, then," said Blue Feather at once. "You are not well enough to walk so fast. And besides, does he know you?"

"I'm not sure. Maybe he does. There!—there he goes around that building."

"Leave him to me," said Blue Feather again, and darted forward in pursuit. He covered the fifty paces to the corner like a hound on a fresh trail, but checked his course just in time to pass around the corner of the building and into the intersecting street at a walking pace, thus avoiding letting the suspected man know that he was followed.

Hubert now proceeded more deliberately, but turned into the other street in time to see Abington disappear around another right-angled turn. Blue Feather was halfway along the square, and the moment their quarry was out of sight again broke into a loping run.

In this fashion the three emerged from the town and went on for a mile or two down the plain below until they came in sight of one of the earthworks that were being constructed as reserve lines of defense in event of a retreat being necessary from the main redoubt at Chalmette. Blue Feather proceeded very much as when stalking a wary buck on the Kentucky hills— moving swiftly when out of sight and much more slowly and not in direct line when he might be seen. Once when Abington came to a full stop and turned about to look behind he saw nothing whatever to alarm him, for the young Indian had dropped like a panther among the grass and weeds, and Hubert was too far away and moving too deliberately to suggest pursuit.

Then, in the behavior of the man they followed, Hubert saw that which convinced him that this counter espionage was no idle matter. It had seemed likely that Abington was bound for the earthwork, and it was possible that he had a message for the officer in charge or some other legitimate errand in that vicinity. But now it became apparent, not only that he had some other destination in mind, but that he especially wished to avoid being seen by any of the men at the breastwork. He was heading diagonally toward the cypress swamp on the east, and he took advantage of every fence and ditch and hedgerow that might assist him in making his way thither without being noticed by the soldiers and workmen. Evidently his anxiety on this score was such as to make him forget entirely the possibility of any one's following directly on his trail, for he did not again pause to look behind him.

A few minutes more and Abington disappeared under the moss-hung branches at the edge of the swamp and far to the left of the breastwork. Seeing this, Blue Feather rose from behind a bush which for a moment had sheltered him and ran swiftly and in a crouching posture along the bed of an empty ditch toward the woods. A quarter of a mile in the rear, Hubert likewise broke into a run. Leaping into the ditch at the point where the Indian had entered it, he made rapid progress to the point where its channel merged into the swamp. Following a fresh trail through the grass and weeds to the right brought him upon Blue Feather again who was lying in the rushes at the end of a long slough or bayou and pointing toward an object just disappearing around a bend deep in the swamp and three hundred yards away.

"There he goes," said the Shawnee. "He had a boat here."

"Oh! I'm *sure* that fellow's up to mischief," cried Hubert in acute vexation. "It's too bad. He'll get away now—unless we can *swim* after him."

"No," said Blue Feather suddenly. "I know where there is a boat, not far from here, that some of the Choctaw scouts have been using. If you can carry one end, maybe we can get it here."

"I'll carry one end of a house, if necessary," declared Hubert, hotly. "Come on. Where is your boat?"

For answer Blue Feather sprang up and started on a run down the edge of the swamp. Hubert kept close behind him, and they soon came upon a small bateau, moored at the end of another bayou, an eighth of a mile below. Blue Feather quickly pulled up the stake to which it was fastened and drew the craft up on the bank. Then the two youths lifted it by bow and stern and hurried with it back to the stream on which Abington had disappeared. By the time their craft was again in the water Hubert was panting like a long distance runner at the end of his course, and the sweat was pouring in streams down his face.

"Never mind," he gasped, as his companion looked at him solicitously, "let's get on. I can rest in the boat."

Without a word Blue Feather seized the oars and was soon swiftly propelling the craft along the turbid stream. The bayou quickly broadened to a wide and shallow waterway, obstructed here and there with fallen logs, overhung by the funereal, moss-engirdled cypress boughs and scarcely to be distinguished from the surrounding areas of swamp. On these a foot or more of oozy water stood that seemed bent on covering and drowning any wholesome life. Thick clouds had covered the face of the sun, and, although the day was but little more than half spent, they moved in this thick jungle among deep shadows that seemed like those of night.

Strange, bright-colored birds flitted silently among the gloomy forest aisles or roosted on the lower limbs, and now and then a snake or a turtle slipped from a floating log and disappeared. It was the eeriest woodland that Hubert had ever entered—one that seemed well fitted to shelter cruel secrets and treacherous crimes. He had barely recovered from the effects of the blow he had received in the night battle, and now, in spite of the breathless haste of his labors with the boat but half an hour before, and the eagerness he still felt to solve the mystery of the tall stranger's behavior, he gradually became conscious of such a damp and deathly chill from these tomblike surround-

BLUE FEATHER SEIZED THE OARS.

ings that he could scarcely keep his teeth from chattering.

On they went, through many turns and windings, for what seemed to be an hour or more, the scout avoiding with wonderful skill most of the water-logged trunks and other obstacles and quickly freeing the little craft from those hidden snags with which it collided in spite of all his watchfulness. Suddenly, as they came around a bend amidst tall rushes, they sighted the bateau of which they were in pursuit, drawn up on a muddy bank a hundred yards away, at a place where a foot or two of rise in the ground formed what might be called an island in the marsh.

Hubert uttered a low exclamation, and Blue Feather dropped his oars and seized his rifle from the thwart. A glance was sufficient, however, to apprise them that the bateau was empty and that no one stood near it on the shore. Only two courses were open to them—to abandon the chase and turn back or to land and search the neighborhood; and, although the latter course was fraught with peril if the strange recruit was really bent on treachery, the two lads spent but the briefest moment in deciding. Their own boat's momentum had by this time carried them a third of the distance to the landing; and now a few more strokes of the oars served to drive its prow up the bank by the side of the other.

Quickly they landed and drew up their boat on the muddy shore. No person was in sight; but now they saw clearly that, beyond a fringe of cypresses and other swamp growth on the margin of the bayou, the space before them was cleared land. A faint track led up through the undergrowth, and on this were plainly discernible the fresh marks of booted heels. Peering from the hedgerow across some two or three acres of dreary, grass-grown opening, the lads discerned a half-ruined cabin of logs and thatch, half covered by a clump of cypress trees. Windows and doors were broken, and the house presented a most desolate and forbidding appearance. It was such a place as might have been, some years before, the haunt of river pirates or runaway slaves.

Fifty yards from the cabin, and almost on the line between it and the watchers by the bayou, was a dismal and sunken stack of hay. The dark gray color of this and the leaning pole at its center indicated that the fodder had been gathered from the field around it some years before and abandoned by its owners as not worth carrying away. Pointing at this object with a swiftly lifted hand, Blue Feather went down on his knees in the grass by the side of the path, and, avoiding the trodden footway, proceeded to crawl toward it. Hubert understood at once that the scout's intention was to approach the house in this manner without being seen by its occupants, and in a moment had thrown himself flat on his stomach and was wriggling snakelike after his companion.

They had approached within thirty feet of the haystack when Blue Feather turned around and laid his finger on his lips. Then he pointed again at the stack and cupped his right ear with his hand for better listening.

Hubert followed his example, and distinctly heard the voice of a man on the other side of the stack speaking in a low tone, but with bitter earnestness:

"I tell you, Captain Balcom, I know whereof I speak. General Pakenham cannot take the redoubt at Chalmette without the loss of thousands of men, if indeed he can take it at all."

Even while his pulses leaped with the purport of the words, Hubert sensed a strange familiarity in the tones. Here again was a voice that he had once known well. He strained his ears for the reply and the name that might accompany it; but the other person was more cautious, and his words were no more than an indistinguishable murmur. The voice of the first speaker quickly followed them:

"And all the while the Chefmenteur Road lies almost open—only a few hundred men and a few fallen trees to defend it. If he will come that way with his main force, while merely threatening the Chalmette works, he can have the city within three days."

At this Hubert raised himself on hands and knees. His eyes gleamed with excitement, and his breath came short and quick like that of a hound on leash that already scents his quarry. Again the reply of the second man was half inaudible. Hubert's eagerness

187

to know his character and mission now passed all prudent bounds. Disregarding his companion's warning frown, he crawled noiselessly yet swiftly forward until the low crown of the stack was all that intervened between him and the speakers.

## CHAPTER XVIII

### THE WAGES OF TREASON

HUBERT had hardly come to a halt in his new spying place when he found Blue Feather at his side. Neither uttered so much as a whisper, and the rank grass around them, being damp with the recent fog and rain, would have given no hint of their coming even to the keenest and most attentive listeners. But the man who had been addressed as Captain Balcom was now replying. His voice was low and his accents broadly English, but in their new position the youths could readily understand him.

"We have lately been told," he was saying, "that nearly the whole of Jackson's force is raw militia, and that many companies are not fully armed. Surely such a rabble cannot stand before veteran troops even with a breastwork to protect them."

"Oh, captain! you forget Bunker Hill," replied the first speaker, earnestly. "I was a young boy, living in Charlestown at the time, and I'll never forget the heaps and windrows of red-coated bodies on that hillside. If the Americans had had but one more barrel of powder, General Howe would never have taken the redoubt. And these Americans here under Jackson—

most of them are backwoods riflemen that shoot far better than the farmers of Massachusetts or than any regular soldiers in the world. I tell you it means disaster to attack them when they stand behind entrenchments."

"You may be right," answered the captain, slowly. "At any rate, I'll tell the General what you say. How far do you think it is by this Chefmenteur way?"

"Twenty miles or more, and much of it through the woods. But a column of light-armed infantry could force its way through in two or three days at most. And the city has no defenses on the northerly side. Look! Here is a rough map I've made that shows the whole situation. Here's Chalmette Plain over here, with the redoubt, and back of it three or four miles, these new earthworks. Down there is the Villeré Plantation where most of your army is now. And over here, don't you see, is the Bayou Bienvenu and the Chefmenteur Road. You can't get artillery through; but think of what four or five regiments of infantry could do, coming on the city from that direction."

"Very well, I'll tell the General and give him this," said the captain. "I believe you're right."

Then the listeners could hear both of the speakers rising to their feet. Evidently the conference was over.

As he lay tensely listening to this fateful dialogue,

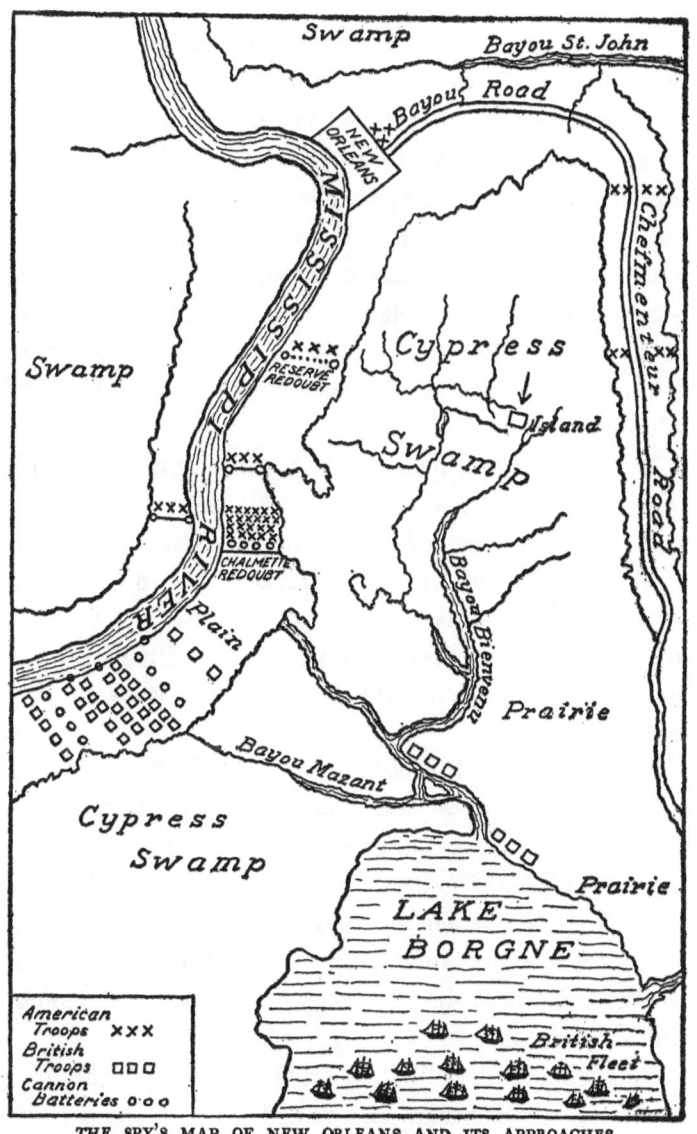

THE SPY'S MAP OF NEW ORLEANS AND ITS APPROACHES.

Hubert had formed a plan in the execution of which he was fully willing to risk his life. The British emissary must never be permitted to reach General Pakenham's quarters, and the traitor who had just given him information which, if acted upon, meant the defeat and ruin of the American army, must be given his just deserts—the noose or the firing squad. A punishment must be meted out to him that would serve as a warning to others of his kind. With his face within six inches of his companion's ear, Hubert whispered:

"We must take them or kill them. You go around one way, and I the other."

Blue Feather nodded full comprehension, and looked to the priming of his rifle. Hubert had no weapon of any sort, but was counting on surprise to give him advantage. Both the lads now stood erect, and, at a signal from Hubert, dashed around the stack in opposite directions.

At the sound of footsteps and the sight of American uniforms the Mobile volunteer gave utterance to an oath of surprise and rage, and, as Hubert threw his arms about him, tried vainly to draw a pistol from his belt. Meanwhile the captain dashed away at full speed toward the other side of the clearing, pursued by Blue Feather whose rifle was leveled at his leaping and twisting figure.

Abandoning the effort to draw his weapon, the volunteer seized Hubert's neck with both hands and tried with all his might to throttle him. The man was surprisingly strong, and might have succeeded in his desperate endeavor had not Hubert taken advantage of the first moment of their struggle to secure a wrestling hold that gave him a priceless advantage. Now the taller and heavier man was lifted bodily and flung backwards. His hold on his enemy's throat was broken, and a second later he found himself prone on his back with Hubert's knee on his chest.

But the victory was far from being won by this triumphant overthrow, for the fallen man, far from acknowledging defeat, twisted and struggled desperately from side to side, striving first to turn and throw the other underneath, and, when that attempt proved unavailing, to draw the pistol which still hung at his side.

For half a minute this furious battle proceeded without a word being uttered. Two shots rang out in quick succession from the bayou beyond the clearing's edge, but Hubert had not an instant's time to think of what they might mean, for the maniacal writhings of his antagonist grew more and more dangerous. Hubert found himself tiring. He knew well that he was in no condition for a trial of endurance, and began to fear that the stranger would succeed at last in drawing and making use of his weapon. Just then he noticed the broken half of a brick which lay on the ground beside them, and over which his opponent's body had repeatedly rolled. Suddenly releasing his hold on the spy's shoulders, Hubert slid his left hand to his throat, then seized the brickbat with the other. Raising it high above his head, he shouted:

"Surrender now. Lie still or I'll *make* you."

The stranger's writhings ceased. For five seconds or more he drew long, panting breaths. Then, his features twisted with a paroxysm of baffled fury, and he roared:

"Go on. Go on, Delaroche. Brain me with that thing if you want to. I'll never surrender."

Again in his tones, in spite of choking rage, those accents so maddeningly familiar!

"You know me, then," panted Hubert. *"Who on earth are you?"*

But even as he spoke he knew the answer. The man in his grasp was the Blue Lighter of New London. Beard and mustaches and long, wavy hair were gone; and both face and figure were much thinner than of old. Only the voice remained as before—that and the tortured eyes of which Hubert had had a last fleeting glimpse in the smoke-filled garden.

"Lucas Windom!" he gasped.

At that moment Blue Feather returned, recharging his rifle as he ran.

"Where is the captain?" asked Hubert.

"Dead," was the reply. "Shall we kill this one, too?"

"No, no!" said Hubert, "we'll make him prisoner.

THE VOLUNTEER SEIZED HUBERT'S NECK WITH BOTH HANDS.

Take off my belt, will you, and help me bind his arms with it."

Blue Feather immediately laid down his weapon and proceeded to do as bidden. When the belt had been fastened, Hubert asked:

"What about that map he gave the captain?"

"I have it here," answered the scout, indicating the pouch at his side.

"Good! Be sure you keep it safely. We may have a use for it. Now let's take this man to the house."

A minute or two later Windom sat on a broken bench, within the half-ruined cabin, with his arms firmly secured behind his back. A hateful scowl was on his face, and his eyes were bent on the floor.

Hubert was thinking hard and painfully. The man before him was a spy and a traitor. He had joined the army of his country only to learn its secrets and betray them. He richly deserved the hangman's noose —the proper wages of treason. Also he was a former valued friend and counselor, a close friend of his kinsfolk in New London—and the father of Margaret. Margaret had declared him the best of fathers and had bitterly mourned his death when they had thought him slain by the rioters. How well Hubert remembered the scene in the cabin of the *Bluebird!* And now was he, her comrade and protector, to join the wolf pack of his enemies and send Margaret's father to a felon's grave?

Some miserable, silent minutes passed. At last, in

low and husky tones, and without looking up, the prisoner asked:

"Where is my daughter?"

"Margaret is safe," answered Hubert. "It seems, Mr. Windom, that you're a spy and a traitor. We heard what you said to the British captain. But I can give you this comfort at least. Your daughter has come to no harm. She is safe and in an honorable home in Virginia."

Windom lifted his head quickly, and, looking piercingly into Hubert's eyes, demanded:

"Is that the truth?"

"That is the truth," answered Hubert steadily. "I do not lie—even to spies and Blue Lighters."

"Blue Lighters!" cried Windom, with terrible bitterness. "That's where it began. Some fools—I don't know to this day who they were—with their signals! And I, a wholly innocent man, tried and convicted by mob law, and suffering worse tortures than the lowest criminal!"

"Do you mean to say that you had nothing to do with the Blue Lights?" demanded Hubert. "That story does not jibe with what I find you doing now."

"So help me God!" cried the prisoner, "I did not know at the time and do not yet know who lighted those signals—or even whether they *were* signals at all. I was tried and convicted by the mob, I tell you; and the verdict was as intelligent and just as such verdicts usually are."

"And are you likewise innocent," asked Hubert, tensely, "of trying to betray New Orleans into the hands of the enemy?"

"No," shouted Windom. "Of that I am *guilty;* and I am proud of it, or rather I *will* be if what you call my treason succeeds. By its treatment of me, this country, that you think so grand and lofty, has earned my everlasting hatred and contempt. I am *at war* with it, if you please to call it so; and I have done and will do everything in my power to inflict punishment upon it."

"I understand you," said Hubert, sadly. "But how long have you felt this way? Was it before I ever met you?"

"No—no! I was loyal enough until that miserable business of the Blue Lights at New London. Though I did hold different views from some of my neighbors as to the wisdom of going to war with England. But when they burned my house over my head and shot me down in the dooryard for an offense of which I was wholly ignorant I made up my mind that if I ever walked again, I'd make them pay a thousand times over. That's why I'm here."

"Well, tell me how you got here?" said Hubert in a gentler tone than he had yet employed. In spite of himself, Windom's story had moved him.

"When I fell down in the garden with that bullet in my chest," answered the prisoner, "the rioters came swarming around me. One of them had a rope; and

perhaps they would have hanged me then and there;
but just then Captain Slocum arrived with half a company of militia and the firemen. They scattered the
rioters, picked me up with the other wounded men,
and took us to the hospital. The house and all my
other buildings burned to the ground. Every one
thought at first that I would die from my wound;
but as soon as they found out I was mending they
got out a warrant, charging me with treason, murder
and I don't know what besides. So I had the pleasant
prospect of leaving the hospital to face a court with
its mind made up in advance to convict me."

"And did they get out a warrant for me also?"
asked Hubert.

"No, they thought of you as having been misled by
me, and therefore not really criminal. Young Bill
Barton, whom you shot down on the side veranda,
occupied the next bed to mine; and as he got better
he used to amuse himself by taunting me with the
prospect of my conviction and hanging. He also
twitted me over and over with your running away
with my daughter, for no one in the town had seen
or heard anything of either of you since the day of
the riot. Then a mulatto cook came from Boston,
where he had landed from a privateer, and told around
New London, so that at last it reached my ears at the
hospital, that you had run away with her on a coast-
ing vessel bound for the West Indies.

"Under these circumstances I didn't mend as fast

as I might. But the day Barton was discharged, and just after he had given me a final volley of taunts and abuse, I formed a plan. I determined to get back my strength as soon as possible, but at the same time to *seem* to be losing ground rather than gaining. I know something of medicine and symptoms, and I succeeded perfectly in fooling the people at the hospital.

"Two weeks later I got possession of my clothes by a trick and, while the doctor and nurse were at supper, slipped out of the window and lowered myself from a balcony. By eight o'clock I was in a rowboat on the lower harbor; and by ten I climbed aboard Admiral Hardy's flagship in the Sound. I told the Admiral what I had been through and what I meant to do. He welcomed the plan, and gave me every assistance. I drilled with the marines every day for five months, so that I might know the trade of a soldier. The fifty pounds I had lost in the hospital were never regained, for hard work and rough living kept me lean. I was landed at Pensacola just two weeks before Jackson reached there with his army. The rest of the story you know as well as I do."

When Windom had finished Hubert made no reply, but for a full minute stood gazing at his prisoner. Blue Feather likewise was silent. He had seated himself on the floor with his rifle across his knees, and evidently awaited his white comrade's decision.

At last Hubert turned to the scout and asked:

"Will you help me, Blue Feather, to deal with this man in the best way I can think of?"

"Yes," said the Indian. "He was your friend, and he is your enemy. You shall decide."

Then, again facing Windom, Hubert went on:

"It may be my duty to take you back to the camp and to tell what I have learned to the proper authorities. ·If so, I'm going to postpone doing it, at least, for if I did take you there, they'd surely put you to death. On the other hand, I certainly am not going to let you go; for then you'd proceed to carry information to the enemy. I'm going to leave you here, with this man to guard you, for a day or two. In that way you can't do any further harm, and I may be able to decide what to do."

Neither of the others made any comment, and Hubert arose to take his leave.

"Have you anything to eat?" he asked the scout.

Blue Feather opened his haversack and showed a scanty ration.

"Well," said Hubert, "I'll be back in the morning with plenty to eat and drink. Till then you'll have to manage as best you can. Good-by."

At the water's edge he found a new perplexity. There lay the two boats, side by side, where they had left them. If now he went away and left one of them there, it might attract the attention of some chance .passer-by and lead to the discovery of their prisoner. After a little thought, Hubert decided to take both of the craft back with him and leave them where they had been before. This course seemed less likely to provoke search and inquiry than any other he could devise. So he pushed both boats into the stream and, tying one behind the other, slowly rowed back through the seemingly endless bayous to the plain.

# CHAPTER XIX

## THE ONSLAUGHT

JUST as night was falling Hubert reëntered the city. Almost the first man he met was Captain Blaisdell.

"Oh, Hubert!" called the captain, "I was hoping to find you. Are you able to help me to-night? Can you take a message to the General at Chalmette?

"Yes, sir. Shall I start at once?"

"Do so. You can get something to eat there; and the General may have some further word for me here. I'll write a note to him now."

Leading the way to his quarters, Captain Blaisdell went to the upturned box that served him for a desk, and in five minutes had written and sealed a letter to the commander. When Hubert had placed this in the breast of his coat, he saluted and would have hurried away; but the captain called him back.

"Wait a minute, Hubert. I've thought of something else. I'll send a man for your horse, and meanwhile we can talk of another matter. How would you like to be sworn in as a regular member of our company?"

"I should like it of all things," replied Hubert warmly.

"Then no sooner said than done. I was thinking of it this afternoon as I came up from the earthwork.

It's nearly a year now that you've been with us; and you've already seen more fighting than many a soldier that's been all through the war. I think the situation here will come to a climax soon; and it may be important to you afterwards to have your name regularly enrolled. Besides, I have some work for you for which you'll need some measure of authority; and I'm going to make a recommendation which will no doubt result in your being made a sergeant. How will that suit you?"

"Why, that's wonderful," answered the lad, his eyes and cheeks glowing with delight. "Can I sign the roll now?"

"Yes," said the captain, producing the document from a dispatch box and handing Hubert the pen. "Your name, right on this line, makes you a soldier of the United States. That may mean something to you later."

Hubert signed his name in a fever of excitement. His ambitions were being realized faster than he had had any reason to hope. Captain Blaisdell was a friend indeed. And, oh!—happy thought! Was he not, of all men, the one to whom he could turn for advice in his sore dilemma in respect to his prisoner? As usual with Hubert, to think was to act. Even as he laid down the pen, he began speaking:

"And now, Captain Blaisdell, I have something very serious to tell you—something on which I want your advice."

"Very well," said the captain, gravely. "Let me hear it."

"I've told you the reason I came away from New London"; began Hubert, "but so far you've never heard the whole story. The man who was accused of lighting those signals—"

Just then there was the sound of hoofs outside, and they realized that the soldier whom the captain had sent for Hubert's horse had returned.

"No. Wait," said the captain, springing up and throwing open the door. "Keep it till to-morrow, Hubert. There'll be plenty of opportunity then; and now I want that letter put in General Jackson's hands just as soon as it can be done. Tell him also that I expect to have the matter concluded so I can get back in the morning."

So Hubert mounted and, after calling at his own quarters for his weapons and water flask, rode away toward the entrenchments at Chalmette. He was delighted with his new status in the army; for he had long been discontented with his rather doubtful rôle of civilian messenger; and the promised sergeancy was a prize indeed. Nevertheless, he was much disappointed at not having been able to carry out his hastily formed plan for consulting Captain Blaisdell with regard to the prisoner whom Blue Feather was guarding. The captain already knew a part of Lucas Windom's story in connection with that of Margaret; and if now he could be told the whole history from the beginning it might be that he could be brought to sympathize with Hubert's present view, and perhaps even to make to the General a recommendation of mercy. As the young soldier made his way in the darkness down the muddy road, and answered the challenges of the sentries, his mind was so filled with the various phases of this problem and with the formulating and rejecting of solutions, that he gave but little thought to his immediate errand or to the situation of the forces he was approaching.

Before he had ridden halfway to the redoubt, however, he became aware that some great movement was near at hand. During the week just past the British had been tremendously active. A day or two before they had succeeded in bringing heavy guns through the bayous to the bank of the Mississippi, and from emplacements there had disabled the American armed vessels on the river. Now, as Hubert suddenly realized, they must have a large part of their army on Chalmette Plain and were at last in position to launch a general assault.

He met several mounted messengers, galloping through the darkness toward the city, and overtook three or four small bodies of troops and ammunition convoys that were making their way toward Chalmette. As he came in sight of the American position and noted the disposition of the troops and guns, he could have no further doubt that an attack was momentarily expected. While the camp ground was

flickeringly lighted by scattered camp fires, and soldiers moved to and fro in the preparation of a meal
or lay at ease on the ground with their arms beside
them, a closely drawn line of infantrymen lay behind
the breastwork with rifles ready for instant use, and
the cannoneers stood by their guns at the embrasures
with their sleeves rolled to their shoulders, with sponges
and rammers ready at hand and matches burning.

General Jackson was mounted and riding up and
down the line, accompanied by two or three officers
of his staff. Hubert delivered his letter and message, and was curtly bidden to wait for a possible
reply. But as the commander immediately busied himself with other matters, and soon rode away toward the
levee with his aides, the messenger, who had eaten
nothing since morning, and now was conscious of a
raging hunger, concluded that there would be no immediate need for his services and that it was time
to make provision for himself. Soon he found a place
among former messmates, who sat around a camp
fire a hundred yards from the breastwork, and joined
them in disposing of generous rations. Half an hour
later, finding himself very tired, and the anticipation
of an immediate attack on the entrenchments having
subsided, he pulled some loose cotton together for a
couch, wrapped himself in coat and blanket, lay down
and went soundly to sleep.

He awakened to a gray and murky dawn, for a
heavy fog was rolling over the encampment. So thick

was the mist that Hubert could hardly see a dozen paces in any direction, and the figures of soldiers moving silently about him seemed those of ghosts or goblins. He made his way to the breastwork, and from there heard the voices of the signalmen, relaying the word from the outposts on the plain beyond that no enemy was yet in sight. Already the frontiersmen had their fires rekindled, and the odors of their cooking filled the air. The line of infantry at the entrenchment had been doubled, and the artillerymen displayed the same readiness for instant battle as on the previous evening. Among a group of officers who now approached on foot from the direction of headquarters at the Macarté mansion Hubert made out the tall, lank figure of the General and heard him say to one of his aides:

"Yes, yes, major, they certainly will. They mean to attack in force this morning. As soon as this fog has lifted so they can see their way they'll be upon us. And we'll be ready for them."

The group passed Hubert without any member of it taking notice of him, and the young soldier concluded that the commander had no present intention of sending him back to the city. He was glad enough to think that General Jackson had forgotten him, for now the great struggle was impending—the climax of the war as he verily believed—and he chose to be on the firing line rather than carrying messages, however urgent, to the rear. Now, hearing at a little distance

209

the voice of Major Harkness who was forming his battalion of Tennessee and Virginia volunteers, he hurried toward him, rifle in hand, to take his place with the Rangers.

General Carroll had command of all this portion of the line; and he was now riding back and forth, twenty paces from the parapet, aligning his forces and calmly distributing advice and commands. Hubert soon found himself with the other Rangers a part of an open formation that was drawn up in four ranks, with six-foot intervals between, and facing the breastwork. The front rank stood close behind the embankment, which at this point was some four feet high and made more difficult of scaling by the deepened canal before it. Most of the frontiersmen in the leading rank rested their rifle barrels on the parapet and thus made still more certain the accuracy of their aim.

"Remember your drill, men," called General Carroll from his saddle behind them. "First rank fires at the word and falls back to reload. Second rank advances to take its place and repeats the maneuver. Then the third and fourth ranks do the same in their turn. When the fourth rank has fired, the first is to have completed its loading and to be ready to take its original place. Thus we will maintain a continuous fire. We've done it perfectly a hundred times on the drill ground. Now let's show the commander that his lessons have been learned, and that we can make use of them in the face of the enemy. Take aim just above the buckles on their crossbelts. And remember—no one, on any account, is to advance beyond the breastwork."

All up and down the line the other officers were repeating these instructions. The men listened attentively to every order given them and promptly obeyed. Grim determination was everywhere visible.

With incredible slowness the minutes went by, and little by little the fog curtain thinned and lifted. When an hour had passed that seemed like ten a faint breeze sprung up and soon was rolling the billows of mist from the plain. The field rapidly grew lighter, and fleeting, yellowish patches appeared on the dark, moist ground. Here and there one could see for a furlong or more in the direction of the enemy, but no armed men were visible save those of the American patrols and signal lines. Faint sounds were heard from farther down the plain—far-carrying voices and the distant thud and clank of heavy wheels; and all at the breastwork knew that beyond that curtain of mist an army was preparing for the onslaught.

Then the wind freshened, sweeping away the fog from half a mile or more of open plain, and revealing, as by theatrical device, the splendid pageant of the British assault. Six hundred yards away, with ready arms and bayonets fixed, and marching as deliberately as on parade, came a scarlet-coated battalion. Now a broad beam of sunlight illumined the faces of the men and glanced from burnished weapons and accouterments. Their formation was four ranks deep and some two hundred files in width, so that they covered a front of two or three hundred yards just opposite the left center of the redoubt where Carroll's men awaited them.

In front of and on both sides of this marching array came mounted officers, resplendent in uniforms of scarlet and gold, and with glittering swords in their hands. Some of their orders now were audible, for the clearing air seemed better to convey the sounds; and from these and the postures of the advancing men the defenders learned that the British leaders were relying for success on the bayonet, the weapon that had won so many hard-fought fields and with which these very men had wrested from Napoleon's veterans the fortresses of Badajos and Ciudad Rodrigo.

A few rods behind this gallant battalion came another scarlet-clad regiment, marching in the same grim order and with the same ready weapons. At a like interval came a third in like array; and more dimly, through the haze beyond them, could be seen the solid ranks of reserves and the carriages of heavy guns.

Suddenly, on Hubert's right, a great gun boomed. Five seconds later this report was followed by the crash and roar of all the cannon on the American line, as when a single thunder peal, after hours of stifling heat and thickening clouds, lets loose a broadside from above that fairly shakes the earth. All around the advancing column spurts of earth told where the shot had struck the ground. Here and there openings appeared in the British line where cannon balls or grape had pierced it; but these were instantly closed, and the marchers came straight on, neither quickening nor retarding their pace, and seeming like men who faced only the pretended dangers of a mimic battle field.

Rifle sights were looked to all along the American line. Some of the Rangers in the rank next the breastwork began taking aim at the oncoming Redcoats and fingering the triggers of their weapons.

"Steady, men, *steady*," came the stern voice of Carroll. "They're still too far away. Wait for the word."

Fifty yards to the left, General Jackson and three of his aides were standing on the parapet, the General studying the advancing column through a telescope. The British guns at the rear of the scarlet line were now replying, making rainbow flashes in the haze, and solid shot came roaring over the earthwork to bury itself in the ground beyond. A second broadside from the American artillery plowed up the field around the marching Redcoats and filled the air in front of the redoubt with billowing smoke.

Again the field was hidden from the sight of the men behind the embankment. General Adair, commanding the sector next to Carroll's, called out, loudly:

"Oh! this smoke is worse than the fog. It will spoil our aim."

"That is true," said the commander when Adair's

words were reported to him. "I'm afraid in that way our cannon will do more harm than good. Go tell these two batteries to left and right here to cease firing."

The cannon were silenced, and soon the air was clear again. By this time the leading battalion of the attackers was within three hundred yards, and the riflemen behind the earthwork were gritting their teeth and fairly straining at the leash. In the midst of a dead silence General Adair pointed at an officer who rode three paces in front of the line, and gave the word to one of his riflemen. There was a sharp crack, and the officer fell headlong to the ground. Instantly the word, "Fire! Fire! Fire!" rang out all along the redoubt, and a roar of musketry rent the air. The front rank fell back to give place to the eager marksmen behind them; and a series of savage volleys sent death and destruction into the close drawn ranks on the plain below.

Twisted and torn by the bullet storm, like a green-leaved tree that writhes in a searing blast of flame, the column wavered and halted, stood for a moment paralyzed, then slowly came on again. More than half the men of the first battalion had fallen, and not a mounted officer remained alive. Now they were within a hundred paces, and the terrible fire continued without a moment's pause. At this close range very few of the backwoodsmen's bullets were wasted. The scarlet ranks went down like grain before a hurricane of wind and hail; the regiment seemed almost to disappear. Then suddenly, and as by one impulse, the scattered survivors turned and fled.

Now the fire from the redoubt was concentrated on the second regiment; and the same terrible scenes were repeated. British soldiers who had never known defeat halted in bewilderment at the frightful slaughter, became blind and deaf to orders and entreaties, and ended by fleeing in panic into the ranks behind them.

· Encumbered with a tangle of fugitives—a broken mob of wounded, weaponless and terror-stricken men which was all that remained of two historic regiments, the third battalion swept forward in its turn. Officers and men alike were evidently determined to scale the breastwork in a rushing charge and come to grips with its defenders. But they also were swept by the hurricane of fire, and in a few incredible minutes were likewise decimated and driven from the field.

Hubert relaxed his hold on his smoking weapon, and letting it lie across the parapet, paused to look about him. The frontiersmen were grimly exultant. Some of them shouted, sang or made coarse jests; but most were silent and breathing heavily as they gazed through the lifting smoke at the field below. Some whom he knew as champion marksmen were quietly engaged in cleaning their rifles and looking to flints and priming pans. Seeing this, Major Harkness called out to the others to do likewise.

"Them Redcoats 'll come on agin, if I know anything

of 'em," he said. "We jest got to be ready. We ain't through fightin' yet."

"There's a lot of 'em out there, major, that'll never come on again," answered one of the Rangers.

At that moment General Carroll halted behind them. He had heard the last remark, and now interposed before the major could reply.

"That's so," he shouted, "but they've got plenty more—eight or ten regiments sure—that haven't been near us yet. Let's not crow too soon. Clean your rifles and see that they're ready to use, for just as sure as we stand here we'll have more work to do."

Carriers now appeared with fresh supplies of ammunition. Each man replenished his stock and looked to his weapon. These preparations accomplished, they were allowed to seat themselves on the ground while a line of lookouts stood behind the embankment and kept watch of the enemy. So passed a few tense minutes. The British artillery still thundered away; but most of its projectiles whizzed harmlessly overhead or buried themselves in the ground in front. In all the fighting of the day thus far Hubert had not seen or heard of the killing or wounding of any American soldier.

Then from the lookouts all along the line came the call: "Here they come! Here they come!"

Every man sprang to his position, and in an instant the ranks were aligned as before. A new and greater attack was being launched. A group of mounted officers led a regiment of Highlanders, tall, brawny men with tartan plaids and swinging sporrans, but armed like their English comrades with the muskets and bayonets they knew so well how to use. Behind them came two more regiments in scarlet coats; and now Hubert could see a second column approaching on the left, on the edge of the swamp, and still another on the right, close under the levee. This attack was far better planned than the first, and supported by greater numbers. Could the American line withstand it, or was New Orleans to prove another Lundy's Lane?

The answer was speedily forthcoming. In the center all the terrible scenes of the first assault were repeated. Officers and men went down before the whirlwind of bullets from the redoubt, and broken fragments of once proud regiments dashed to the rear like herds of frantic cattle running from the wolves. On the left and right the British columns, protected somewhat by the clouds of cannon smoke, actually reached the American defenses. But at the eastern end of the line General Coffee with his Tennesseeans and the Choctaw scouts who fought waist deep in the water of the swamp, and on the western extremity the Regulars and the Louisiana companies beat back the Redcoats with well-aimed volleys while themselves suffering but trifling loss. Less than a score of British officers and men ever mounted the breastwork; and these instantly fell from the parapet, their bodies pierced with numberless wounds.

With the scarlet-coated regiments broken and fleeing before them, the savage exultation of the frontier soldiers threatened to burst all bounds. All along the line the riflemen sprang up on the embankment, and, recklessly exposing themselves to enemy bullets or cannon shot, continued frantically to load and fire.

"Down there, men! *Down!*" came the stentorian call of the commander. "Keep back of the breastwork."

Most of the men within hearing of his voice obeyed the order. And the General turned to his staff officers and said:

"Pass the word all along the line to all company officers to make their men observe order and keep their ranks behind the works. The British still have strong reserves, and if they meet our men in the open field, *we may be beaten yet.*"

The aides departed to right and left on this errand; furious shouts of command were heard from the captains; and soon the line of dare-devil figures disappeared from the parapet. But now the last of the advancing British regiments broke and withered under the hail of lead from the redoubt. A yell of triumph went up from the frontiersmen; and one young fellow leaped up on the embankment, flourishing his long hatchet and shouting:

"Come on, boys! Follow me! Let's get at 'em."

The men in the rear ranks raised a cheer and surged forward toward the breastwork. A spasm of rage swept over the General's face, and he clutched at his waist in search of his pistols.

*"Down, sir, down!"* he shouted in the voice of a lion. For a moment the youth hesitated, then sprang back to his place in the line. Finding no pistols in his belt, the general borrowed a pair from an aide. Then, with one heavy weapon in either hand, he sprang up on the parapet.

"Now," he said, with a steely glitter in his blue-gray eyes, and in a voice which no man who heard it would ever forget, "I'll shoot the first man who dares go over the works. *We must have order here.*"

No word was heard in reply, and the ranks instantly resumed their ordered alignment. Out on the plain below the last act of the tragedy was being played. Scattered groups and individuals from the broken regiments were running madly toward the rear or desperately seeking shelter behind mounds or ditch banks, still pursued by the deadly rifle fire. The British guns still vainly belched and roared, and those on the right and left of the American line replied.

Hours went by, while the sun climbed slowly overhead and declined in the west, and the backwoods riflemen still held their places and grimly awaited another challenge. But no more scarlet-coated regiments appeared. As night approached the cannon fire from both sides grew intermittent, and finally ceased. The Battle of New Orleans had passed into history.

## CHAPTER XX

### THE PRISONER IN THE MARSH

ON the following day Hubert tried his best to find opportunity to go to the island in the marsh where he had left Blue Feather with his prisoner. They had neither provisions nor blankets, and might by this time be suffering severely for the want of them. But Major Harkness and General Carroll found so many occasions to employ him that he had not ten minutes of leisure from dawn until dark. The second day bade fair to be like the first. Further supplies of various kinds were needed at the redoubt; and there was much to do for the wounded and the prisoners. He rode twice to the city on urgent commissions and returned with messages that would not brook delay.

Captain Blaisdell had not been with the Rangers at the Battle of New Orleans; and Hubert had wondered many times what could possibly have detained him. Now he learned from the major that Captain Blaisdell had received orders on the night before the assault to assemble a company from the reserves at the city and march down the west bank of the river to reënforce General Morgan, who, with a few hundred militiamen and half a dozen guns, was holding some hurriedly made defenses. These were a little to the rear of the principal American position and separated from it by the width of the Mississippi.

General Pakenham's assault in solid columns on the redoubt at Chalmette was in reality not so planless and foolhardy as it seemed. Very early in the morning he had dispatched Colonel Thornton with a thousand or more of infantry and marines to take the works on the west side and turn their guns to sweep across the river to the flank and rear of the American redoubt. According to the plan now reported by some deserters from the enemy, the volleys from this captured artillery were to precede the advance of the British regiments on the plain; and it was expected that they would throw the frontier militiamen into confusion and make comparatively easy the capture of the position.

But Colonel Thornton's expedition encountered a variety of unexpected obstacles and delays; and, although his companies finally arrived before the American position and actually captured the works and drove away their defenders, their success was too late by hours to produce any effect on the main conflict, for the great assaults on the redoubt at Chalmette had already been delivered. The outcome was that Colonel Thornton shortly received orders to fall back from his advanced position, which had now become a dangerous one, and under cover of night managed to recross the river.

# THE PRISONER IN THE MARSH

Among the wounded prisoners whom he carried to the main British encampment was Captain Blaisdell. Hubert received this news with bitter sorrow, for he could well imagine the miserable lot of a wounded man under such circumstances; and he racked his brains to discover some means by which he could be of assistance to his patron and friend. To the anxiety aroused by this situation on the captain's own account was added Hubert's further perplexity in relation to the prisoner in the marsh. He had hoped for the captain's assistance in finding some honorable solution of that problem. There was no one else in the army to whom he could confidently apply; Major Harkness was distractedly busy with the affairs of his command and some extra duties that had been thrust upon him; and Lieutenant Green, who was temporarily in charge of the Rangers, was for some reason out of favor with the General. To Hubert it gradually became evident that any action taken must be wholly on his own initiative.

At two in the afternoon he managed to get permission to leave the camp on errands of his own. Riding posthaste to a large farmhouse which he had observed on his many journeys, he procured a supply of food and carried it, stowed in a sack, to the head of the bayou where he had left the bateau. To his inexpressible relief, the boat had not been disturbed. Tying his horse in a thicket near by, he stowed his provisions and rifle in the craft, seized the oars and pushed off into the gloomy aisles of the swamp.

Half an hour later he arrived at the island, and made all haste to the cabin. There sat Blue Feather with his rifle on his knees, very much as he had left him three days before; but Windom was stretched on a couch of hay, his body covered by an old, torn coat, his eyes tense and glittering, and his face flushed and swollen with fever.

Blue Feather, hearing the tremendous firing in the direction of Chalmette, had readily surmised the reason for Hubert's delay. On the day of the battle he and his prisoner had had nothing to eat; but at noon of the day following the young Indian had concluded that Hubert would be still further detained, and had managed to leave the island and procure the necessary provisions himself. First binding the prisoner hand and foot, and closing and barring the door upon him, he had explored the country on the farther side of the clearing and ended by finding a path which led for several miles, through the swamp and across bridges of fallen trees, to the open plain. He had procured some bread and cheese and potatoes at the very farmhouse which Hubert had just visited, and returned safely with them to the island. These supplies, with some old clothing which he had also secured, had relieved their most pressing necessities; but their only drinking water was that of the bayous; and it was to this fact that the scout attributed their prisoner's present condition.

## THE PRISONER IN THE MARSH

Hubert's stay at the cabin was brief. Windom scarcely addressed a word to him; and even when Hubert, speaking directly to him, promised to return on the following morning, if possible, with fresh water and medicines, he only gave surly and half-intelligible replies. On the other side of the couch Blue Feather touched his forehead significantly, and Hubert understood that he believed the unfortunate man was already light-headed with the fever. With a heavy heart the young soldier said good night to the cabin's occupants and relaunched his boat for the return journey. If Lucas Windom were to die thus miserably, while he held him prisoner as enemy and spy, what a pitiable close that would be to a life that had had its full measure of suffering, and which, after all, had not been devoid of good intent! And what account could he ever give to Margaret of her father's end?

On the next day it was impossible to return. The British were slowly withdrawing their forces from before the redoubt at Chalmette, but there was no surety that General Lambert, who had succeeded to the command when his superiors, Pakenham and Gibbs, were slain in the assault, would not attempt to retrieve the disaster by other and better-planned attacks. The Redcoats still had the advantage in numbers and equipment, and it seemed altogether likely that some new thrust would be delivered—perhaps by the Chefmenteur Road —the repelling of which would call for every ounce of strength the American forces could muster. In these anxious days, what with dispatching scouting forays to gain the latest news of the enemy's movements, providing for the sick and wounded of both armies, and securing ammunition and supplies, Old Hickory seemed never to sleep; and all his aides and messengers were in the saddle from dawn to dark and many hours afterward.

As he rode on these various errands or joined in the performance of necessary work at the redoubt, the problem of his prisoner was never absent from Hubert's mind. Above all things he longed for the opportunity of discussing it fully and frankly with Captain Blaisdell; but the thought of that brave and generous man— now perhaps dying of his wounds in the camp of the enemy—only added grief and distraction to his perplexity. Once he fully resolved to seek out Major Harkness, and, as a matter of life and death, make him listen to the spy's piteous history. Perhaps then he could induce him to intercede with the commander. But for an American officer to feel any measure of sympathy with Lucas Windom in his present plight it would be necessary for him to believe, as Hubert did, that the prisoner had been innocent in the matter of the blue lights and hideously wronged by the mob that had assaulted him. And when Hubert visualized the attempt to make the hard-headed old frontiersman believe that one who had just been caught red-handed in an act of treason was guiltless of any previous wrongdoing his resolution failed. Utterly despairing

225

of the success of any such effort, he returned to the search for ways and means to guard his dangerous secret.

It was three days before Hubert could again visit the island. This time he carried a two-gallon can of fresh water and a supply of quinine and other medicines as well as bread and meat and vegetables. The prisoner was, if anything, more ill and listless than before; and though he was fully conscious, it was clear from what little he said that he was utterly indifferent whether he lived or died. His grandiose scheme of revenge having wholly failed, he apparently had no further interest in life. Lying on his couch of moldy hay, under the miserable old coat that served for a blanket, and with a ten days' growth of gray and straggling beard on his face, he was indeed a pitiable object, and Hubert could not look at him without a revulsion of feeling that almost amounted to nausea. Even so he did not forget that Windom had himself told of the stratagem that had made possible his escape from the hospital at New London; and he took Blue Feather outside the cabin to warn him against any similar deception which might result in their prisoner's slipping from their hands.

But now as the days went by there came sifting through the camp and the city persistent rumors of peace. Just as, three months before, the seemingly airborne tidings that the great British attack was in preparation had pervaded the whole southwest, so now, from like mysterious sources, came the message that the war was at an end—that the treaty was already signed in Belgium and that all the invading forces would soon be withdrawn. General Jackson, deeply fearful of a slackening of morale in his army, sent forth definite denials that any such news had been received; but the rumors were repeated nevertheless. The soldiers grew restless and began to ask their officers when they would be led homewards, and there were mutterings in the city and in the legislature against the martial law which was still rigidly enforced by the commander.

Hubert's fourth visit to the cabin in the marsh came after a week's interval, during which time, in spite of the urgency of his other duties, his prisoner's desperate plight was always the subject of his thoughts. At first sight of him it seemed to Hubert that his worst fears were fast being realized. The spy's countenance had lost its flushed and swollen look, and had become yellow and shriveled like that of a victim of famine on a plague-stricken, tropical island. His eyes held an unnatural glitter, and while he called frequently for drink, Blue Feather said that he had eaten nothing for two days or more. It was evident that under these conditions and without medical aid he could not long survive; and for the first time his captors openly discussed their dilemma before him. They must take him where he could be cared for, and that very soon, or he would certainly perish.

Suddenly the sick man interrupted them. In a hollow voice, that yet was startlingly loud in that lonely place, he said:

"There is no need for you to argue and contrive. Who am I to burden you in this way? There is your gun ready loaded. Put the muzzle to my head and blow my brains out. Then you can be sure that I will give no more information, and may take yourselves back to your camp in peace."

Hubert stood for a moment gazing at his prisoner— a moment tense and painful beyond anything he had ever known. Then he fell on his knees beside the couch and took one of the fevered hands in his.

"Mr. Windom," he said, tremblingly, "we will do no such thing. We will—we *must* find some way to save your life."

"Yes," answered the other, bitterly, "save me from swamp fever, and turn me over to the firing squad!"

"No," cried Hubert. "We'll not do that either. I know at last what is the right thing to do. It's come to me this moment. If you'll give me your word of honor not to give any information to the British leaders which can be used against us, and never again in any way to make war against your country, we'll take you back to their camp and release you."

"How can you do that?"

"We can find our way to Lake Borgne by way of these bayous; and we'll leave you within sight of one of their outposts. You are to leave the United States and never to return. Come now, will you give us your word?"

"Yes," answered Windom, slowly, a faint color overspreading his yellowed countenance, "and, though it may have a strange sound to speak of the word of honor of a spy, I think that you know that mine may be relied upon. You will let me have news from my daughter?"

"Yes, she is at the Blaisdell plantation, near Norfolk in Virginia. After the peace is signed you may write to her there; and, if she chooses to do so, she may join you in England or in Canada. And now do you feel able to make the journey to the British camp to-day?"

"Yes, it must be to-day or not at all, I think. Just give me another drink of water, and I will be as ready as I can be."

Hubert induced him to take a cup of milk instead. After a little time, much enheartened by the improvement which this nourishment and the new hope of freedom had brought about in the prisoner's appearance and manner, he hurried out to assist Blue Feather in preparing a fresh couch of hay in the bottom of the boat. This accomplished, they lifted the sufferer, laid him at full length upon it and covered his lean body with the overcoat.

Then a new difficulty arose. The boat was not large enough to carry safely all three of them. Hubert was the last to get aboard; and his weight brought the gunwale of the little craft dangerously close to the water.

"This is too much weight," said Blue Feather. "We cannot go this way. But, after all, why should you go at all? I know the way to the great channel and from there down to the lake. It will be better, anyway, for you to go back to the camp at once, for otherwise there might be many questions asked."

After a moment's thought Hubert concluded that the scout had suggested the only practicable plan. So, after wringing Windom's hand and wishing him Godspeed, he stepped ashore. Blue Feather quickly gave him directions as to the path which he had followed on his journeys on foot to the plain, then pushed off and started down the stream with his passenger.

The boat had not proceeded a hundred yards when Hubert, who still stood among the flags watching it, saw the scout drop his oars and seize his rifle from the thwart beside him. Windom raised his head and peered into the overhanging bushes on the bank, and while the boat drifted toward them Blue Feather held his weapon ready for instant use as he might have done at the entrance to a wild beast's den.

Presently the bateau disappeared into the little cove among the trees, and Hubert was left gazing after it in a fever of suspense. Two minutes later it reappeared, and, turning directly away from its previous course, came rapidly back toward the landing.

"What is it?" asked Hubert in a tense whisper as soon as the craft drew up beside him.

"A boat," said Blue Feather. "Some one has landed on the island here."

"Who are they?"

"I cannot tell. No one is in sight. But the boat was not there this morning. I think I must land there and trail them. Otherwise we cannot tell who they are or what they will do."

"No, I don't think I'd do that," answered Hubert, hurriedly. "I'm afraid if we delay you won't be able to reach the outposts to-day. And we're leaving the island in any case. After all, these people may be the owners of the land or some one else who has a better right here than we have."

Blue Feather shrugged his shoulders.

"Very well then. If you think best, we'll pay no attention to them. But I can never rest when there are folk near me about whom I know nothing. I suppose it is the way of my people."

"If we don't trouble them, they won't trouble us, I think," said Hubert. "Still, I'll walk down that way, keeping even with you as you row; and if there are people about who mean mischief, we'll find them."

He sprang back to the edge of the clearing while the scout again turned the prow of his boat in the direction of the great bayou. Following the fringe of brush and trees, Hubert soon came on the stranger craft, so snugly placed among thickly overhanging trees and bushy margin growth that he wondered greatly at Blue Feather's observing it. There was no one in its neighborhood, however, either on the bank or in the clearing beyond; and when he had searched the growth at the margin for a hundred yards farther he called to the young Indian through an opening in the flags to tell him so.

Turning away, Hubert proceeded at once to search out the path Blue Feather had described; and by means of it, in an hour's time, regained the open plain a mile or two above the redoubt. It was late afternoon when he reëntered his tent at the encampment. He was deathly tired; and now, for the first time in weeks, no urgent tasks awaited him. So he threw himself on his bed, and in a few minutes fell into a heavy slumber.

It was dark when he was awakened by the entrance of two soldiers, one of whom seized him by the shoulder and shook him roughly.

"What do I want?" jeered the intruder in reply to Hubert's angry remonstrance. "I want *you* to get up and come along with us. You're under arrest, by the General's orders."

"Under arrest?" was the amazed response. "What for?"

"Oh, it's well enough for you to say 'what for?' but I reckon you know well enough. It's for *spying* for one thing. I heard that much."

"And are you going to take me to the General?" said Hubert, sitting up on his couch and staring in bewilderment at his accuser.

"No sir, we're not. We're goin' to take you back

to the city, and lodge you safe in the jail there. Them's orders. And now shut up and come along. We've talked too much already."

Clearly there was nothing for it but to obey. Gathering his few belongings, with the exception of his weapons which he was directed to leave where they were, Hubert marched before his captors to a mule-drawn wagon on the outskirts of the camp and climbed aboard among a motley collection of thieves, drunkards and deserters, white and black. The soldier on the driver's seat whipped up his team, and the two guards mounted their horses and followed close behind. By seven o'clock the cavalcade reached the town and drew up in the jail yard. The prisoners were marched into the low building, hurriedly searched and assigned to their quarters.

Scarcely realizing what had happened, and still incredulous as to the General's orders, Hubert found himself thrust into a dark and evil-smelling place, and heard the key turn in the lock behind him.

Evidently he was charged with a serious crime—spying, the guard had said—and no doubt that interpretation was being placed on his behavior toward Lucas Windom. Too late he realized that the boat hidden in the rushes at the island had, as Blue Feather suspected, betokened the nearness of dangerous enemies.

Exhausted as he was with the labors and anxieties of the day, Hubert lay for half the night on the rude prison cot, endlessly and vainly revolving in his mind

233

the details of his situation. Would he be given opportunity to explain the dubious course he had chosen, or would he be led forth at sunrise to that lonely point behind the levee where traitors paid the mortal penalty? To this grim question and to a hundred others that now besieged him he could find no answers. As he lapsed into unconsciousness at last, only one thing was clear—he was General Jackson's prisoner, credibly charged with aiding the enemy; and General Jackson, when he faced a hostile army, tolerated no thoughts or feelings save those that led toward victory.

# CHAPTER XXI

## THE STAR WITNESS

FOUR days later a guard came to the prison and conducted Hubert Delaroche to the old mansion where the commander had established his city headquarters. In a large inner room which had evidently been a parlor, but which was now roughly adapted to its present use by the introduction of a large oaken table and tiers of filing boxes, the general sat busily examining and signing papers. Of these a great, disorderly pile had accumulated, some portions of which threatened momentarily to slide from the table to the floor. At the General's side was a trim young officer in a captain's uniform, and in a shadowed corner of the apartment, at the left of the door, stood a wounded man whom Hubert, in the partial dusk, after the bright sunlight of the streets, failed to recognize.

The young soldier entered the room with high-held head, and saluted the commander exactly as though he were reporting for some special duty. He well knew that serious charges were pending against him; but he had formed no plan for meeting them except that of telling the simple truth. Utterly unconscious of any wrongdoing, he refused to believe that any possible

235

train of circumstances or the malice of enemies could so conspire as to thrust upon him the status of a criminal. He knew that military punishments were swift and severe; but all his observation thus far had confirmed his belief that they were invariably bestowed upon those who deserved them.

The General looked up from his papers and fixed the youth before him with a stern and piercing gaze.

"You are Private Hubert Delaroche," he barked.

"Yes, sir."

"You are charged with treasonable communication with the enemy, and with aiding the escape of a spy."

"Of the first I am not guilty; and as to the second I have something to say in explanation. The man—"

The General held up his hand to stop him, and cried out harshly:

"Hold on! Hold on now. It's my duty to warn you of the nature of this examination, so that you may proceed with your defense with full knowledge. This is not a court-martial. That will come later; and at that time you will be entitled to the benefit of counsel, for the officer in charge will appoint some one to defend you. This is merely an informal inquiry, held to enable me to decide how to proceed. You have the right to refuse to make any statement here; and I warn you that any statements you do make may be used against you. Under these circumstances, do you wish to tell your story here, or do you prefer to wait until you can be advised by your counsel?"

"I'll tell it here," said Hubert steadily. "It will be the same story wherever I tell it."

"Very well, then," said the General, the lines of his face slightly relaxing. "We'll hear the other side first so that you may understand what is alleged against you; and then you may make whatever statement you think best. Private MacBean!"

"Yes, sir," said the man in the corner, advancing toward the desk with a salute to the commander. As he passed he favored the prisoner with an ugly leer, and Hubert recognized his old enemy of the New London streets and of the interrupted fray on the camp ground. Evidently the wound or fracture he had sustained in the night battle a month before was still unhealed, for his left arm was still sustained by a cotton sling, the folds of which had grown dingy with long use. His uniform was dirty, his eyes bloodshot, and his whole person exhaled the odors of cheap tobacco and alcohol. But he was perfectly sober, nevertheless, and carried himself with the assurance of one who well knew the part he was to play. Failing to best his enemy in fair fighting, he had lodged charges of treason against him. No doubt he would put the worst aspect on all the facts he knew; and if these were not enough, to such a witness perjury would be no obstacle. For the first time Hubert clearly realized what it meant to be the object of such a fellow's hatred.

The General frowned slightly as he observed the man before him. "Go ahead," he said. "Tell everything that has a bearing on the case; but don't waste our time with anything else."

"Well, it was this way, General," began MacBean in a loud, confident tone. "This feller here was livin' in New London a little over a year ago, where I lived. He lived with some Peace Party folks named Brewster that we thought'd bear watchin'. Well, there was a man there named Windom—a Peace Party man too— always shoutin' 'bout the war bein' wrong and so on. And he burnt those Blue Lights that stopped Decatur gettin' out er the harbor. You see—"

"I know about the Blue Lights. How do you know he burned them?"

"Well, we knew well enough. We saw him comin' back from there where they was burnin'. And the next day I saw this feller here, Delaroche, comin' away from his house, and I warned him 'bout not goin' there any more because Windom was known to be a spy. But the next day after that the' was a crowd went to Windom's house and set fire to it. This feller here was in the house at the time, and he tried to fight off the crowd; and he shot a feller named Barton. But they finally had to run for it, 'cause the house was burnin'; and Windom got shot down, but this feller got away. Run off with Windom's daughter, girl 'bout fifteen years old. None of us ever saw anything more of him until six weeks ago here at New Orleans.

"Now the man named Windom, he fooled 'em at the

238

hospital—made 'em think he was worse hurt'n what he was; and one night he got away. And the next thing we see of him he turned up around here too—workin' as a spy for the Redcoats."

"When did you see him first?"

"Well, it was out in the swamp down here, jest the other day. You see, I was 'spicious of this feller here —I knew well enough he was a spy, too—and I kind of kep' watch of him. Once or twice lately I seen him go to a farmhouse down here and come away with stuff to eat and drink and so on, and then he'd take a boat in the swamp there and row away with it. I couldn't foller him, and didn't know nothin' of where he went, only I was sure he was up to some mischief. So the other day I got a feller to help me—a half nigger named Brentford—an' we got hold of a boat on the bayou there. We kep' watch, an' sure enough, this feller come along with some more provisions. He started off into the swamp, same as ever, but this time we trailed him.

"He went to a kind of island place, 'way out in there, and went into an old cabin the' was there. Me'n the nigger hid our boat in the bushes, and then we crawled up through the grass and got in under the floor of the house. There was cracks in the floor, so we could hear what was goin' on. There was three fellers there. This feller, Delaroche, an Injun they call Blue Feather that's supposed to be a scout for us here, and another man that was sick.

"We couldn't hear jest all that was said, and I couldn't make out who the sick man was till finally I heard Delaroche call him by name. It was this Windom, the Blue Lighter. We could make out enough of the talk so't we learned that he'd be'n spyin' for the British 'round here right along, and now he'd fallen sick, and this feller, Delaroche, and the Injun scout had the job of takin' care of him.

"Windom's rich, I guess. He's got plenty of money some place; and he offered each of 'em five hundred dollars if they'd git him back safe to the fleet. They argued on that for a while; but they finally agreed on it. They was to take him back to the British lines in a boat; and that's jest what they did."

"Why didn't you interfere?"

"Well! The' was two of them, an' they both had their guns. I didn't have any gun, of course; and Brentford didn't want to tackle 'em alone."

"And did you see the sick man plainly?"

"Yes, sir, we did. When they took him out to the boat, we see him plain. It was that same Windom, sure enough."

"Very well," said the General after a moment. "You may stand back. And now, Delaroche, what have *you* to say?"

Hubert drew a long breath, stepped forward to the table, and, looking the General fairly in the eye, began his story. He told in full detail of the Blue Lights episode as he understood it, the fight in the street with

MacBean and his helper, the battle at the Windom house, the shooting down of Windom, and his own and Margaret's escape to the schooner. Then, more briefly, he related the events of the voyage, Brentford's desertion, the arrival at Norfolk, the visit to the Blaisdell plantation and the other events that led up to his presence in the army at New Orleans. From the point at which he first noticed the Mobile volunteer the narrative became fuller, and all the events with which this individual had been concerned for the past four weeks were clearly and completely told.

There had been no interruption thus far, and no sign on the General's face of either belief or disbelief. But when the narrative reached the point where Hubert decided on the spy's release both of the men on the other side of the desk leaned forward and stared at the speaker in amazement; and the great, sinewy hands of the commander gripped the edge of the board as though he throttled some dangerous beast.

"Heavens and earth!" he exclaimed at last, "Didn't you know you were committing a military *crime* in letting that man go?"

"I knew that if I didn't he'd die," said Hubert.

"Huh! Much you ought to care if he did. He was a spy, wasn't he?"

"Yes, sir. But I thought the time was past when he could do serious harm, even if he broke his word to me."

"I don't know about that. We're liable to be attacked again, any time. And just what did he say about money?"

"Not a word. There never was any talk of money between us."

The General averted his eyes from Hubert's steady gaze and for a long minute sat looking at the floor, his breath coming and going as though he had been running on an uphill road. None of the others spoke, and the General had just lifted his head to address the prisoner again when there was a sound of hurried footsteps without and a high, tenor voice was heard in the anteroom:

"I'm looking for a fellow named MacBean. Somebody said he was here."

Then the lower tones of the orderly in reply:

"He is here, doctor. He's in there with the General now. You can see him when he comes out."

"Well, I wish I could get hold of him right away. I'd like to tell the General something of him. Is that boy, Delaroche, in there, too?"

At this point the speaker was interrupted by General Jackson himself who had risen from his desk and now stood in the open doorway:

"Come in, doctor. Come right in."

The doctor entered, and when he had closed the door behind him, the General inquired:

"What was it about MacBean? What did you want to tell me?"

"Oh, there he is!" cried the doctor exultantly, as he

caught sight of the star witness in the corner. "I've been hunting the camp over for him. I heard this morning that he'd brought some kind of charges against this young man here, Delaroche. I don't know what they are; but I *do* know that he hates Delaroche like poison; and I'm willing to bet my last dollar that his charges are a pack of lies. That man—" and here the surgeon pointed his forefinger at MacBean like a pistol and advanced threateningly toward him, "that man is a *liar* and a *skulker*. I wouldn't believe anything he said if he swore to it on a stack of Bibles."

MacBean visibly quailed before the little surgeon's denunciation. The latter stood glaring at him as though the informer were a cowardly and vicious hound that might attack him if his back were turned.

"Well, what is it he's done, doctor?" asked the General. "Let's hear about it."

The surgeon wheeled about toward him.

"I'll tell you the whole thing, sir, and you can judge for yourself. He was in the night attack on the British, down near the Dominguez Canal—the first brush we had with them in this campaign. And he came to me about nine o'clock in the evening with what he called a wound through his arm. It was a little scratch on the flesh of his upper left arm, not half an inch deep at the most, where a bullet had grazed him. I had lots of them that needed my attention ten times worse; but I stopped to bathe the scratch and wrap

243

it up just because he seemed to think it was so terrible. There was nothing to prevent his going right back to his company; but he went and sat down with the wounded instead. And towards morning, when we got the wagons going toward the city with some of the worst hurt of the men, I saw him riding away in one of them. If I hadn't been at that moment taking care of a man who was likely to bleed to death, I'd have chased up that ambulance myself and made him get out of it, because there were half a hundred lying on the ground there who needed the best care we could give them, and his riding in that way meant that one of *them* had to be left behind.

"Well, sir, I forgot all about this fellow until yesterday when I happened to see him with his arm in a sling. I asked a man in his company whether MacBean got hit in the big assault; and he said no, that his arm had been fractured or something like that *in the night battle,* and he'd had to carry it in a sling ever since. Then I knew right away what he'd done. He'd gotten all the fighting he wanted that first night; and he meant to keep out of any more. He'd fixed up that sling to make every one think he was disabled; when, in fact, there was almost nothing the matter with him. Let's examine him now and see whether I'm right."

"I tell you," burst out MacBean, "that wound is a good deal worse'n you say. I can't use my arm at all."

"Well, we'll see," said the General, grimly. "Undress the arm, doctor."

The surgeon seized the scowling witness, removed the arm from the sling and deftly unwound the bandages. When the flesh was exposed an already healed scar came to view—a little, red furrow, some two inches long and half an inch wide, where the thin, newly-formed skin revealed the color of healthy tissue beneath.

"Bah!" cried the doctor. "What did I tell you? He might have gotten a wound like that while picking blackberries for his grandmother. And Delaroche here had five times as bad a hurt in that same scrimmage, and he's been working and fighting ever since."

The General smiled broadly.

"That's all right, doctor," he said. "Thank you for your information, which has indeed some importance under the circumstances. We won't need to keep you longer."

The doctor opened the door and passed out into the anteroom. MacBean started to follow him.

"You will remain, MacBean," said the General, sharply. "We're not through with you yet."

MacBean slouched back to his corner; and the commander turned to his aide with the roughened brow of one who vainly tries to remember some detail that has escaped him.

"We had something else, didn't we, captain, in this Delaroche case? Were there any other witnesses?"

"No, sir," replied the captain, promptly, "but there were some papers. There's a statement from Major Harkness; and there's also a letter which came in for the prisoner last night, and which you directed me to hold."

Quickly locating these papers in the pile before him, he handed them to his superior.

The General bent his brows on the first for a minute or two; then looked at Hubert gravely:

"The major gives you a good character," he said. "And, from him, that means something. Now let's see about this letter."

The missive was still in the envelope, and the general carefully cut this open with his penknife. The address was in a round, girlish handwriting which Hubert instantly recognized.

"Hum!" said the reader, "from Margaret Windom, Blaisdell Plantation. Is that Captain Blaisdell's place in Virginia?"

"Yes, sir," replied Hubert.

The letter was of many pages, and for three or four minutes the commander continued to read without comment or change of expression. Then by degrees a warmer look appeared and a broad smile spread over his rugged countenance. He laid down the missive and slapped the table resoundingly.

"Ah! young blood! young blood!" he cried. "No wonder you didn't want to hang her father! I was young once myself, and I've not forgotten it. *You're*

246

*a lucky dog, sir.* Nice, sweet-hearted girl like that! I'll wager she's pretty, too. And she doesn't say so in so many words, but a blind man could see where *her* sun rises and sets."

Then, half shouting: *"Look out you deserve it, sir,* and *continue* to deserve it. If you *don't.* . . . By the Eternal! I'll hunt you up, wherever you are, and make you sorry."

Hubert hardly knew what to say in reply, although he felt quite sure that the old soldier's thunder blast was not meant as a condemnation. Presently the General began speaking again—and now there was a twinkle in his eye.

"Well, where were we? Oh, yes, there's one thing more. Delaroche, did you find our jail here a pretty good jail as jails go?"

"I can't say I enjoyed my stay, sir," answered Hubert, smiling. "I've never slept before in a place that smelt so badly."

"Still," insisted his questioner, "it's a pretty good jail, isn't it? And that cell you had—good strong walls, dependable lock and so on?"

"Yes, sir, I can say that for it. It was strong enough to hold *me,* anyway."

"Well, that's it. A good cell like that ought not to stand idle in these busy times. You're not going back there, but *I know who will.* Captain," he went on, his voice and manner suddenly altering, "see that that fellow there, that liar and skulker, MacBean, is taken at once to the jail and put in the cell that Delaroche has been occupying."

The tones were as loud and rough as those of a ship captain in a gale of wind. There could be no doubt that Old Hickory meant just what he said. The captain rose, saluted and proceeded to carry out the order. With hanging head and glowering eyes, MacBean marched before him. A moment later his footsteps and those of his guards were heard on the pavement without.

The General rose, took Margaret's missive from the table and handed it to Hubert.

"Here's your letter, boy. Sorry I had to read it," he said heartily. "And now I can tell you something in strict confidence. I believe you were right in thinking that that man, Windom, couldn't do us very much harm even if he broke his word to you. We have had no actual dispatches, but I believe these reports we've been hearing are true, and that the commissioners have already signed a treaty of peace. That's why I don't need to enforce the letter of the law in this matter, and can pass over your rather glaring breach of discipline. But remember now, not a word of that to anybody."

"I will remember," said Hubert warmly.

"Very well, then. And I will say that you have had somewhat hard usage for a man who has gone through what you have and who actually saved us from the consequences that might have ensued from that advice about the Chefmenteur Road getting through to the enemy. Major Harkness says you've been recommended for a sergeancy; and I'll have to see if we can't do a little better than that. Now that's all for to-day. And if you get into any more trouble, come straight to me."

Hubert saluted and passed from the room with the sensation of walking on high-floating clouds. Now for the first time he knew the real Andrew Jackson, and he did not regret any phase of the experience by which the knowledge had been acquired.

# CHAPTER XXII

## YOUTH AND DREAMS

Thorn River Valley, Kentucky,
March 10, 1815.

HUBERT DELAROCHE,
  To Mistress Margaret Windom,
    Blaisdell Plantation,
      *via* Norfolk, Virginia.

MY DEAR MARGARET:

I wrote you from New Orleans in February that
the war was surely over and that we might soon be
starting for home. On the nineteenth came the news
that the treaty had been signed, and the next day all
of us of the Ranger Troop and many other companies were ordered north. At Knoxville we were
mustered out; and now the captain and I hope to be
at the plantation some three or four days after this
letter reaches you.

There are some things I can write you now that
Captain Blaisdell asked me not to write about before,
as he feared it would make Mrs. Blaisdell worry. He
was wounded and captured by the British on the day

of the great battle. Ten days afterward, when they were withdrawing toward their ships, he managed to escape in the confusion, and got into the great swamp that runs for miles on the east of the river below New Orleans. He wandered there for two or three days, and nearly starved to death. Then Blue Feather found him. Blue Feather had been scouting near the British lines; and he found him lying unconscious on the ground, and brought him back in his boat.

The captain was very weak, and a little out of his mind with fever; and it was three weeks before he was out of danger; but now he's well and his wound has healed. We've come up here to the Thorn River Valley, which was an old camping place of the Rangers, partly because the doctor told him to go into the mountains for a little while to get the fever thoroughly out of his system and partly because he is so good as to want to help me carry out a plan which I have had in my head for a year, and which I'll tell you all about.

But first there are one or two more things which happened at New Orleans of which I haven't written you, because they really need so much explanation that they are much better told than written. The first is a splendid piece of news for you. Your father is not dead. He got better of the wound he had at New London, and later escaped from the country. I can't tell you just where he is now; but I have every reason to believe he is alive and well, and that he will

write to you before long. He thinks of you **very**
often.

I wrote you about John MacBean and how he got
sent to jail for shamming wounded so as to keep out
of the fighting. Just a day or two before the peace
dispatches came he was tried by court-martial for
cowardice and drummed out of the camp.

In my last letter I told about being promoted to be
a sergeant. Well, the very day of the peace news I
got a great, thick envelope from the General, and found
I was made a lieutenant in the United States Army.
He said when I went to thank him, "Oh, that's just
something to carry home with you to show your folks
you didn't waste your time here." Everybody in the
army says he's the most wonderful general we've had
since Washington, that he saved the Mississippi Valley
for the United States, and that he will surely be president some day.

And now about our errand up here in Kentucky.
When I first came to this place a year ago I thought
it was the loveliest I had ever seen, and how wonderful it would be to have a home here some time.
Just before we started north I said something of this
to Captain Blaisdell; and he went right to the General with it. The result is that Colonel Winchester,
who was on the General's staff and had been a member of the legislature of Kentucky, came up here with
us; and they're having five hundred acres surveyed
for me to file on and half as much for Blue Feather

right next to it. Colonel Winchester is making all the arrangements because the General tells him to. Most any officer or soldier in the southwestern army would do anything in the world for General Jackson.

I'm going to build a house on the very spot where this camp stands, and some day have the finest place in eastern Kentucky. There are already quite a number of settlers at the Forks, five miles below here, and the colonel says there will be a town there before long because it's a natural crossroad. General Jackson is going to give me some blooded colts from the Hermitage.

But first I'm going home to Massachusetts and finish my education. I'll go back to Cedricswold, and maybe I can enter Harvard in the fall. Then it will be only four years before I can return to Kentucky. Blue Feather will live on the land meanwhile and take care of it for both of us. He's here with us now, and has just brought in a deer.

Oh, you ought to see this place when the sun is just coming up over old Saddleback. Then all the bush and fern is dripping with dew, and there are a million little rainbows along the edge of the intervale. And such a woodsy fragrance—just like the Berkshire Hills in partridge-hunting time! Blue Feather and I were out for three hours yesterday morning, and brought in pigeons and turkeys enough to last us a week. The stream is full of trout, though they won't take the bait just now; but even if there were no fishing at any time, it's worth a great deal just to look at. It's all colors from white on the stony slopes to brown and black in the pools, according to the state of the sky and the way the light strikes it. A furlong below the knoll there was a beaver pond a few years ago, and I can easily dam it up again, so we can keep a boat there and maybe run a little mill.

And then you should see the valley in the evening when there is a moon. It's just like the pictures you have seen of fairyland. There is a grove of big sugar trees that reminds me of one, half a mile from Cedricswold, that I visited with my older brothers one moonlight night when I was six years old. I thought then and for years afterward that there was nothing like it anywhere in the world.

Now I'm coming to the special reason for this letter. I want you to help me persuade the Blaisdells to come up here with us for a week or two before I start for the north. Of course, the captain will want to stay home for a fortnight or so, anyway, but can't we so manage things that the whole family will want to come up here before I have to leave?

By that time the leaves will be starting out on the hardwoods and all the forests will have that purplish tinge that comes over them in the springtime in the mountain country. Right now the streams are running bank full; the ground in the woods is all spangled with early blossoms; and the geese are flying northward. There's nothing like it down in the flat lands.

## OLD HICKORY'S PRISONER

You tell the girls about it, and get them to talk to their mother. It will be the most wonderful time for all of us.

I want you to see this valley—see the long meadow at the foot of this knoll, the blue hills up beyond and the pine woods. And when you have seen it, as it will be in April, both by daylight and by moonlight, you will know perhaps whether or not this is the place in which you would choose to spend a lifetime.

(1)

**THE END**